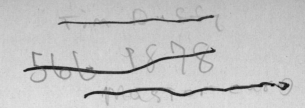

KONRAD

CHRISTINE NOSTLINGER, who was born in a suburb of Vienna in 1936, is the critically acclaimed author of ten novels for young readers. She lives in Austria where she works on a Viennese daily newspaper.

KONRAD

CHRISTINE NOSTLINGER

TRANSLATED BY ANTHEA BELL
ILLUSTRATED BY CAROL NICKLAUS

AN AVON CAMELOT BOOK

5th grade reading level has been determined by using the Fry Readability Scale.

Originally published in German as *Konrad*, Copyright © 1975 by Verlag Friedrich Oetinger, Hamburg.

AVON BOOKS
A division of
The Hearst Corporation
959 Eighth Avenue
New York, New York 10019

Translation Copyright © 1976 by Andersen Press Limited
First British edition Copyright © 1976 by Andersen Press Limited
First American edition Text Copyright © 1977 by Franklin Watts, Inc.
Illustrations Copyright © 1977 by Carol Nicklaus

Published by arrangement with Franklin Watts, Inc.
Library of Congress Catalog Card Number: 77-7489
ISBN: 0-380-62018-9

The Franklin Watts, Inc. edition contains the following Library of Congress Cataloging in Publication Data:

Nostlinger, Christine.
  Konrad.
    SUMMARY: By mistake, an unconventional lady receives a perfectly behaved factory-made child in the mail. To escape being returned, he must learn "normal" child behavior.
    [1. Parent and child—Fiction 2. Humorous stories]
  I. Nicklaus, Carol. II. Title.
  PZ7.N672K03   [Fic]   77-7489

First Camelot Printing, January, 1983

KONRAD

Chapter One —————

Mrs. Bertie Bartolotti was sitting in her rocking chair having breakfast. She had three cups of coffee for breakfast, two rolls with butter and honey, two soft-boiled eggs, a slice of brown bread with ham and cheese and a slice of white bread with liverwurst. Since Mrs. Bartolotti rocked back and forth as she ate—after all, rocking chairs are meant for rocking in—she got brown coffee stains and yellow egg stains on her light blue bathrobe, and bread crumbs fell down the neck of her bathrobe too.

Mrs. Bartolotti stood up and hopped around her living room on one foot until all the crumbs inside her bathrobe had fallen right down to the floor. Then she licked the honey off her sticky fingers. "Well, my dear," she told herself. "Get washed and dressed like a good girl, will you, and then you'd better start work. And get a move on!"

Mrs. Bartolotti went into the bathroom. She felt like having a nice hot bath, but unfortunately the goldfish were swimming about in the bathtub. There were seven little goldfish and four big goldfish, and Mrs. Bartolotti had taken them out of their bowl and put them in the bath the day before, to give them a change of scene. After all, thought Mrs. Bartolotti, other people go away on vacation, but those poor fish have to spend their whole lives swimming around and around and around in a circular goldfish bowl. So Mrs. Bartolotti decided to make do with a nice warm shower.

Before she left the bathroom Mrs. Bartolotti put on a lot of bright makeup and looked at herself in the mirror over the sink to see if she looked young or old. Some days she was young, some days she was old. This was one of Mrs. Bartolotti's young days, and she was pleased with her face. "I do look young! Really young and pretty!" she told herself appreciatively.

Mrs. Bartolotti never told anyone how old she was, so no one knew, and that meant she was several different ages. Old Mrs. Miller, who lived next door, called her "young Mrs. Bartolotti" when she mentioned her. Little Micky, old Mrs. Miller's grandson, called her "old Mrs. Bartolotti." Mr. Thomas, who sold cosmetics and toothpaste and ointments in his drugstore, and had two deep lines on his forehead from reading so many prescriptions, said, "Bertie Bartolotti—she's a woman in the prime of life!" Mr. Thomas was in the prime of life too. He was fifty-five years old, and he and Mrs. Bartolotti used to meet twice a week. Once a week he visited her, and once a week she visited him. They would go to the theater or the movies, and then they went out for a meal, and then they went somewhere else for a glass of wine, and then they went to a coffee shop. The two days when they were friends were always Saturday and Tuesday.

When she had looked at herself in the mirror long enough, Mrs. Bartolotti went back to the living room, sat down in her rocking chair again, and wondered whether to start work now, or go shopping, or perhaps go back to bed. Just as she had made up her mind to go back to bed the doorbell of her apartment rang. It was a very long, loud ring. Mrs. Bartolotti jumped, nervously. That was the way mailmen and Western Union men and firemen rang the doorbell.

Sure enough, it was the mailman standing outside the door ringing the bell so loud and so long, but he was not delivering a letter. He was delivering a parcel. He was puffing and panting, and he wiped his brow. "Weighs a ton!" he said, pointing to a large parcel wrapped in white paper. "Well, at least half a ton!" He dragged the parcel through the hall and into the kitchen, and Mrs. Bartolotti signed a receipt and gave him fifty cents. The mailman said, "Good-bye," and Mrs. Bartolotti said, "Good-bye," and went to the door to see him out.

Then she sat down on a kitchen chair in front of the big white parcel. She plunged her hands into her hair, which was dyed blonde, and sat there thinking, "What on earth can it be?"

Mrs. Bartolotti stood up and walked around the parcel, looking for the name and address of whoever had sent it. She didn't find any name and address, not even when she tipped the parcel over carefully and looked underneath.

Mrs. Bartolotti found her kitchen scissors and cut the string around the parcel. Then she tore off the white wrapping paper, and next she removed the lid of the big carton she found inside. Under the lid were some sky-blue shavings.

Mrs. Bartolotti began digging around among the sky-blue shavings. She could feel something smooth, hard and cold under them. She flung them out of the carton, and then she saw a huge, gleaming, silvery can. It was about the height of a man's umbrella, and as thick as the trunk of a thirty-year-old tree. There was no label on the can, only a sky-blue dot about the size of a nickel. One end of the can had TOP on it, and the other end had BOTTOM, and there were letters around the middle of the can saying: *All documents will be found inside.*

Mrs. Bartolotti rolled the can out of its carton and stood it upright, so that the end saying TOP was on top and the end saying BOTTOM was at the bottom. She rapped the side of the can; it sounded hollow.

"Can't be fruit cocktail," she muttered.

"Could be popcorn," she added.

Mrs. Bartolotti was very fond of popcorn. But when she took a closer look at the can she realized it couldn't be popcorn either. Indeed, it could not contain anything that was runny or crumbly, because it was the kind of can that has a strip of metal all around the middle and a ring-pull to open it. If you pull the ring you can rip off the strip of metal all the way around and the two halves of the can come apart. So obviously there was something solid inside this can!

"Corned beef!" said Mrs. Bartolotti to herself, taking hold of the ring-pull. Mrs. Bartolotti liked corned beef even better than popcorn. Forty pounds of corned beef go a long way, and Mrs. Bartolotti knew she could never get all that into her refrigerator, but she thought, Never mind, I'll give five pounds to Thomas, and I'll give old Mrs. Miller another five pounds, and I'll give little Micky ten pounds. What's more, I shan't have to go shopping for a whole week, thought Mrs. Bartolotti. I'll have corned beef for breakfast and lunch and tea and supper. . . . And she pulled the ring.

There was a funny hissing sound. When Mrs. Bartolotti had finished pulling off the metal strip, the top half of the can was hanging askew over the bottom half, and the hissing stopped. There was a smell of carbolic and hospitals and fresh, ozone-laden air.

"That's no way for corned beef to smell. Unless it's very poor quality corned beef," muttered Mrs. Bartolotti, lifting the top half of the can.

It was a very good thing the kitchen stool was right behind Mrs. Bartolotti, because she got a considerable shock. She started trembling from the bleached ends of her hair down to her toenails, which were painted bright green. She felt quite dizzy. She swayed, and collapsed onto the kitchen stool.

The creature who was crouching inside the can said, "Hello, Mom," and gave her a friendly nod.

Now, when Mrs. Bartolotti was very scared she didn't just tremble and feel dizzy. When Mrs. Bartolotti was really scared stiff she also saw little golden stars dancing in front of her eyes against a pale violet haze.

And at the moment Mrs. Bartolotti was scared absolutely rigid. She saw the little golden stars dancing, and she saw the pale violet haze, and behind that she saw the lower half of a can with a crumpled-looking dwarf inside. She saw a crumpled-up head with a very wrinkled face, and crumpled-up arms, and a crumpled-up throat and a crumpled-up chest. Then she saw a crumpled-up abdomen too, because the dwarf, who must have been sitting down inside the can, stood up. He said, "The nutrient solution is inside the lid, Mom."

Mrs. Bartolotti shook her head and blinked her eyes rapidly, in an effort to get rid of the little stars and the violet haze. Sure enough, the little stars went away, and through the violet haze she could see a sky-blue packet fastened to the top half of the can. It bore the words NUTRIENT SOLUTION, and underneath it said, in smaller letters: *Dissolve contents in six quarts lukewarm water and apply to the contents of the can immediately after opening.*

One corner of the packet said, "Tear here," with an arrow pointing to the right place. Mrs. Bartolotti tore the corner off where the arrow showed.

"Please hurry," said the dwarf, "because I can't stand much open air without the nutrient solution."

Mrs. Bartolotti got up from the kitchen stool, swaying slightly, took the pink plastic bucket out from under the sink and put it under the faucet. She found a jug which she knew held one quart and poured six jugfuls of water into the bucket, adding the nutrient solution too, of course. The nutrient solution was dark brown. Mrs. Bartolotti stirred the mixture with a wooden spoon, and the water in the bucket turned light brown.

Then Mrs. Bartolotti slowly and carefully poured the light brown water over the head of the crumpled-up dwarf. She expected the water to run off him, like a shower, and splash into the can and over the floor. But she was wrong. The crumpled-up dwarf soaked all the light brown water up, getting less and less wrinkled all the time, and soon he did not look like a dwarf anymore, but like a perfectly normal child.

And when Mrs. Bartolotti had poured all six quarts of solution over him, she saw a little boy standing in the can. He seemed to be about seven. He had healthy golden skin, very smooth and soft, and pink cheeks, bright blue eyes, white teeth and fair, curly hair. He had no clothes on.

The little boy climbed out of the can and handed Mrs. Bartolotti a sky-blue envelope. Mrs. Bartolotti took the envelope. It was made of plastic, sealed at the edges to keep it watertight, and it bore the word DOCUMENTS in big black letters.

Mrs. Bartolotti took her kitchen scissors and cut the envelope open along the dotted line. It contained a birth certificate and various records of inoculation and vaccination.

The birth certificate said:

Father: Konrad Augustus Bartolotti
Mother: Alberta Bartolotti
Born: 23 October 1967
Place of birth: Unknown

And the inoculation records showed that Konrad Bartolotti had been inoculated against scarlet fever, whooping cough, TB, dysentery, diphtheria and tetanus and vaccinated against smallpox.

Then Mrs. Bartolotti found something else in the envelope: a deckle-edged card covered with ornamental writing in blue ink. It said:

Dear Parents:
   Your dearest wish has now been granted.
   We, the manufacturers, wish you every happiness, and hope you will be completely satisfied with your

child. May he always bring you joy, and fulfill the expectations you have of him and of our company.

Our company has done all in its power to provide you with a satisfactory, promising and good-natured child. The rest is up to you!

We are sure you will encounter no difficulty, since our goods are particularly easy to handle and control, and, being the products of a highly developed technology, are quite free of those faults or defects that can occur in nature.

Finally, we have a request to make. Our product is constructed in such a way that it needs affection as well as the usual methods of child care and upbringing. We ask you to bear this in mind.

With every good wish for the future.

Yours sincerely,

The signature looked something like "Monbert" or "Honbert."

Chapter Two

Mrs. Bartolotti looked at the seven-year-old boy whose name, according to the birth certificate, was Konrad Bartolotti. His teeth were chattering, and he had goosebumps.

"Don't you have any clothes to put on?" asked Mrs. Bartolotti.

"They said I'd get some clothes here," said Konrad.

Mrs. Bartolotti fetched her thick knitted jacket from the closet in the hall and put it around Konrad's shoulders. Konrad's teeth stopped chattering.

"They told us styles change very fast," he said, "and people wear different things every year, so there wouldn't have been any point in giving us clothes in advance!" Konrad looked at the sleeves of the bright pink jacket, which were far too long for him. "Is this the style for boys of seven now?" he asked.

"Heavens, no!" said Mrs. Bartolotti. "Little boys wear very different sorts of things. That's my jacket. The fact is, I didn't know . . ."

"What didn't you know?" asked Konrad.

"Well . . . I didn't know they were sending you."

"But we're only sent if someone orders us!"

Mrs. Bartolotti thought she detected a touch of reproach in Konrad's voice.

"Did the Sales Department make a mistake?"

Mrs. Bartolotti thought she detected a touch of sadness in Konrad's voice.

"No, no!" said Mrs. Bartolotti, hastily. "The Sales Department didn't make any mistake, certainly not, only— only I didn't know you were coming today! I thought it wouldn't be for another week or two.

"Are you glad I'm here, Mom?" Konrad asked.

Mrs. Bartolotti looked at Konrad. Needs affection, she thought. Well, of course he does—everybody needs affection! And he's very nice, too, thought Mrs. Bartolotti. I'm sure he's as nice as Thomas, and every bit as nice as old Mrs. Miller. And he can hardly help being a lot nicer than old Mrs. Miller's grandson Micky. And I *must* have ordered him, sometime or other. So now he's here, and he needs affection. . . .

"Yes, I am very glad indeed you're here, Konrad!" said Mrs. Bartolotti.

Konrad smiled. Then he said he was rather tired after the can opening, because can opening is a strenuous business, and he asked if he could lie down and sleep for two or three hours, because he was supposed to do that, or there might be subsequent damage.

Mrs. Bartolotti took Konrad into her bedroom. She cleared the magazines and newspapers and the romance she was reading and the cookie box and a bag of candies off her bed, swept the crumbs off the bedspread and plumped up the pillows.

Konrad got into bed. Mrs. Bartolotti covered him up, and he fell asleep at once. But before he fell asleep he said, "Good night, Mom!" and Mrs. Bartolotti realized that she really did like Konrad. She liked him a lot.

Mrs. Bartolotti drew the shades down over the windows and tiptoed out of the bedroom, closing the door quietly behind her, sat down in her rocking chair and took a big cigar out of her cigar box. She needed a cigar badly, to soothe her nerves. When Mrs. Bartolotti had inhaled the cigar smoke deeply three times, the pale violet haze finally went away. And when she had inhaled three more times, she remembered that a very long time ago, when she and Mr. Bartolotti were still living together, she really had wanted a child.

"But surely I'd have remembered ordering one!" Mrs. Bartolotti said to herself.

"Well, you forgot ordering a hundred pounds of thumbtacks too," she told herself, and then she answered herself back, very irritably, "Don't be silly! Thumbtacks are not the same as children! I'd never have forgotten ordering something so unusual!"

She went on arguing with herself for some time, and finally agreed with herself that Mr. Bartolotti, now a thing of the past, must have sent in the order for the child, probably to give her a nice surprise. Mrs. Bartolotti was rather touched, because generally speaking, Mr. Bartolotti had never given her nice surprises.

And when Mrs. Bartolotti had smoked her cigar down to a tiny stump, she remembered a time, years and years earlier, when Mr. Bartolotti had kept asking whether a parcel had arrived for him. He had kept on about it for at least three weeks.

"Of course!" said Mrs. Bartolotti. "That was it! He must have been expecting our child at the time. I see it all now!"

Mrs. Bartolotti got out her change purse, her wallet, her

little leather bag and her plastic folder. The change purse contained only a few coins. There were three twenty-dollar bills in her wallet, for the rent. There were some quarters and nickels and dimes in the little leather bag. Mrs. Bartolotti counted them. The plastic folder contained six twenty-dollar bills for emergencies.

"Well, my dear, I'd call this an emergency," Mrs. Bartolotti told herself. She took off her bathrobe, went into the bathroom, whisked a pair of jeans and a T-shirt off the line and put them on.

The jeans were still a bit damp around the zipper and the waistband, and as they had not been ironed they were as stiff and creased as only unironed jeans can be. The T-shirt had not been ironed either, and it was not the very latest style.

Never mind, thought Mrs. Bartolotti, no one will notice if I put a coat on over them.

Mrs. Bartolotti only had one coat, a thick, pale gray fur coat. She put it on, though it was a very warm day.

"And if I'm wearing my fur coat I need my fur cap," said Mrs. Bartolotti, cramming her big fur cap on her head. Then she stuffed the six emergency twenties, her change purse, her wallet and the little leather bag into her pocketbook, called for a cab and left the building.

Mrs. Bartolotti asked the cab driver to take her "downtown." In the city where she lived you said "downtown" when you meant the center of the city, where all the big stores were.

Although it was early October, and so it was fall really, the weather was quite warm. Mrs. Bartolotti was sweltering inside her fur coat, and people stared at her in the street because she was wearing it. But Mrs. Bartolotti was perfectly used to being stared at. She usually wore some item of clothing that struck other people as peculiar. Either it was wrong for the time of year or it was wrong for the occasion she wore it to. Mrs. Bartolotti would go to play tennis in black pants, or wear jeans for an evening at the opera, or go down to the market for milk in a long silk dress, or wear her climbing gear to go to the movies.

"You're just trying to annoy people," Thomas the druggist said, but he was wrong. Mrs. Bartolotti did not want to annoy anyone; it was just that she put on the first clothes that came to hand. Or perhaps she might suddenly feel like wearing red, and since her climbing pants were such a lovely bright red, she would go and put them on.

Mrs. Bartolotti spent an hour going around the stores, and at the end of it she had spent most of the emergency twenties and was carrying nine plastic shopping bags full of children's clothes. She had bought undershorts and socks, printed and embroidered T-shirts, corduroy pants, leather pants, a belt and an Indian-silk shirt. She had bought three pairs of slippers, red with violet stripes, in sizes 10, 11 and 12. One pair is sure to fit, she thought. She had bought a gorgeous cap, too, made of pale blue leather with silver and gold embroidery and a little golden bell on top. And she had bought a jacket which was all different-color patches.

Mrs. Bartolotti had spent so much money that she felt she ought to economize now, so instead of taking a cab she walked home. (She hated traveling by bus.) She happened to pass a toy store, and it struck her that a child would be in urgent need of toys, so she took her wallet out of her pocketbook, took out the rent money and bought a big box of blocks, a little teddy bear, a picture book, a jump rope, a plastic gun, a doll that could say MAMA, a dancing man on a stick and a woolly elephant.

Next Mrs. Bartolotti happened to pass a furniture store, and she realized with a start that Konrad needed a bed of his own. She took her change purse and her wallet and her little leather bag out and counted up all the money she had left. It seemed just about right. She went into the store and looked for a child's bed. She found a red one that had a green mattress with white elephants on it. The red child's bed was the most expensive bed in the store, and the green mattress was the most expensive mattress in the store too.

Mrs. Bartolotti paid for them out of the money she had left, and the sales clerk promised that they would be delivered that afternoon.

Mrs. Bartolotti was almost home when she realized that Konrad would need candy and ice cream, so she took out her change purse, with the last of her money in it, and went to the baker's and the candy store. She bought a bag of taffy, a bag of sugared almonds, a pint of raspberry ice cream, a dozen packets of bubble gum and ten lollipops.

Konrad was not in bed anymore when Mrs. Bartolotti got home; he was standing by the living-room window wrapped in a sheet, looking down at the road.

"Hello, Mom," he said.

Mrs. Bartolotti dropped all eleven shopping bags, took

off her fur coat, threw her fur cap on the table and wiped her hot forehead.

"Hello, Konrad," she said, wondering whether that was the right thing to say to a boy of seven, or whether you just kissed them instead. Or hugged them, anyway. Or patted them on the shoulder. She realized that she knew very little indeed about boys of seven. But she had often seen old Mrs. Miller picking up her grandson Micky and kissing him on both cheeks, so she went over to Konrad and picked him up in the air. Now they were face to face.

Konrad looked at Mrs. Bartolotti, and suddenly she was not quite sure whether he wanted to be kissed. So she put him down again. Konrad went on looking at her.

"Why did you pick me up and then put me down again?" he asked.

"I was going to kiss you," said Mrs. Bartolotti, "but I wasn't sure if you'd like it."

"Children get kissed by their parents when they've been good," said Konrad. He licked his upper lip, frowned and half closed his eyes. You could see he was thinking hard. After a while, glancing down at the sheet wrapped around him, he said, "I was alone at home, and I didn't break anything or do any damage, but I did take the sheet off the bed and wrap it around me. Only I hope that wasn't being naughty, because I felt cold."

"Of course it wasn't naughty!" Mrs. Bartolotti assured him.

"Then I suppose you can kiss me," said Konrad.

Mrs. Bartolotti picked Konrad up in the air so that they were face to face again, and she kissed first his left cheek and then his right cheek. Konrad's skin was warm and soft and smooth, and Mrs. Bartolotti enjoyed kissing him, so

she kissed his left cheek again, and then his right cheek again, and then she put him down on the floor. After that she went to get the shopping bags and started to unpack her purchases.

"Do you like this?" she asked, taking a T-shirt embroidered with spangles out of one of the bags.

"Do you like this?" she asked, taking a leather belt with an enormous brass buckle shaped like a bull's head out of another.

Every time Mrs. Bartolotti took something out of the shopping bags and asked Konrad if he liked it, he nodded —but Mrs. Bartolotti couldn't help noticing that he did not nod very enthusiastically.

"I don't think you really like any of these things," she said sadly.

"Oh, yes, I do," said Konrad politely. "Of course I do. If that's what you like I'm perfectly happy!"

"But I wanted to get things *you* would like!" said Mrs. Bartolotti. "Come on, let's try them on you!"

Konrad hesitated. Then he said, "I don't really know what the style is now. Only . . ." And he stopped.

"Only what?"

"Only . . ." Konrad stopped again.

"What? Please tell me!"

"All right, I will if you want me to," said Konrad. "I spent quite a long time looking out the window, and I saw quite a few children, and some of them were about my age —and they weren't wearing things like these at all."

"What sort of things did they wear, then?"

"Gray pants, and striped or checked shirts, and blue or brown jackets."

"That's because people are so dreadfully dull!" cried

Mrs. Bartolotti. "Because they don't have any imagination, and they can't think of anything new and they're scared to even try!"

And Mrs. Bartolotti thumped her chest, right where she had a big golden sun, a pink stag and a green cat painted on her T-shirt.

"Now look at me!" she said. "*I* don't wear the same sort of things as other people! I painted the sun and the stag and the cat on this T-shirt myself, with a special fabric paint. I'm the only person in the whole world with a T-shirt just like this, and proud of it! Pretty, isn't it?"

"I don't know," said Konrad.

Mrs. Bartolotti sighed. Then she said, "Well, all right, I know everyone isn't the same as me, and the people who are different from me are right in their own way too. If you like, I'll buy you some blue pants and a checked shirt and a blue jacket tomorrow, all right?"

Konrad shook his head and said that would be a waste of money, and anyway there was no need. He pulled on the red and white checked underpants, pulled the T-shirt with the colored spangles over his head and pulled on the pair of purple corduroy pants with the green heart-shaped patches over the knees. Then he fastened the leather belt with the big brass buckle shaped like a bull's head around his waist, and put the pale blue cap with the little golden bell on his head.

"You look great! Fantastic!" cried Mrs. Bartolotti, delighted. "You're the nicest-looking child I've ever seen in my life!" And Mrs. Bartolotti tried to take Konrad to look in the mirror in the hall.

"Come on!" she said. "Come and see how nice you look!"

"No, thank you," said Konrad. "Boys of seven shouldn't look in the mirror except when they're washing their ears and brushing their teeth, in case they get vain and conceited."

"Oh. Sorry," muttered Mrs. Bartolotti. Suddenly she remembered the raspberry ice cream. "Heavens to Betsey, the ice cream will be melting," she cried.

She took the carton of ice cream out of the shopping bag, carried it into the kitchen, opened it and turned the contents out onto a glass dish. She got a box out of the kitchen cabinet. The box contained long, thin wafers, and she stuck them all around in the mound of ice cream. It looked pretty, like a porcupine with very long prickles. Mrs. Bartolotti carried the glass plate with the ice cream porcupine into the living room and put it down in front of Konrad.

"Look!" she said. "You'll like this. It's very nice."

"Aren't people only supposed to eat ice cream in summer?" asked Konrad.

"Dear me, no!" cried Mrs. Bartolotti. "People can eat ice cream any time of year! I like eating ice cream best in winter, and I like it best of all when it's snowing outside."

"But I thought ice cream was only for dessert," said Konrad.

"Oh, my poor lamb, I'm so sorry!" said Mrs. Bartolotti. "I quite forgot how hungry you must be! Shall I make you a ham sandwich? And you can have a soft-boiled egg, and I'll get out the pickle jar."

"No, I'm not hungry," Konrad explained. "The nutrient solution gives me enough nourishment for twenty-six hours. I just thought people weren't allowed to eat ice

cream if they hadn't finished up all their meat and vege-
tables first."

"Goodness gracious me, why do you keep asking what
people are *allowed* to do and what they're *supposed* to
do?"

"That's how a boy of seven ought to behave," said
Konrad.

"But I haven't the faintest idea what boys of seven are
allowed to do or aren't allowed to do!" cried Mrs. Bartolotti, at her wits' end.

"Well, never mind about the ice cream for now," said
Konrad. "But you could find out tomorrow when people
are supposed to eat ice cream, couldn't you?"

Mrs. Bartolotti nodded, though she had no idea just
where she could find that out. One way or another she
was getting rather confused—so confused that she ate up
all the ice cream and all the wafers, and got a stomach-
ache and a frozen throat.

Konrad sat opposite her, watching her eat the ice cream.
Now and then Mrs. Bartolotti stopped and held a spoon-
ful of ice cream or a wafer out to Konrad, asking if he
wouldn't like to try it, but he just shook his head.

When Mrs. Bartolotti had finished the ice cream, Konrad asked how he could help with the housework, and if
she wanted him to wash the dishes, or vacuum the apartment, or take out the garbage.

"Do you enjoy that sort of thing?" Mrs. Bartolotti asked
him.

"I don't know if I enjoy it or not," said Konrad. "But
boys of seven are old enough to do those things, and it's
their duty to help their mothers by doing little jobs around
the house."

"Yes . . . yes, of course," said Mrs. Bartolotti. But then she decided there was still plenty of room in the garbage can, and the dust wasn't very thick yet, and there were still several clean plates and spoons and cups and dishes in the kitchen closet, and she said she'd rather Konrad played with his new toys.

Konrad picked up the big box of blocks, took the top off and looked at them.

"What lovely colored blocks!" he said. Mrs. Bartolotti heaved a sigh of relief. "You can build towers with them," she said. "Or a whole train, or a town hall, or even an airplane!"

Konrad put the lid back on the box. "Where can I play?" he asked.

"Where?" Mrs. Bartolotti didn't quite understand.

"I mean, which is my play corner?"

Mrs. Bartolotti had never heard of a play corner before.

Konrad explained that all children had either a playroom or a play corner, and as there wasn't any playroom in Mrs. Bartolotti's apartment, could she let him have a play corner?

Mrs. Bartolotti thought. She had a living room, a workroom, a bedroom, a kitchen, a hall and a bathroom, and each room had four corners, making twenty-four corners in all. She said Konrad could have any corner he liked. Or if he'd rather, he could have all twenty-four. Or he could have the middle of the room too, she added.

"Thank you very much, but one corner is quite enough," Konrad said.

"Well, choose whichever you like, then," said Mrs. Bartolotti.

"Where would I be the least nuisance?"

"Nuisance to who?"

"You."

"You won't be a nuisance to me at all, really you won't! As far as I'm concerned you can play anywhere."

"Then I'll play in this corner," said Konrad, pointing to the corner of the room between the window and the door into the hall. "Is that all right?" he asked. Mrs. Bartolotti nodded. Konrad put the box of blocks on the floor, took the top off again and looked at the blocks.

"I bought a lot of other things too," said Mrs. Bartolotti hopefully. "Look, there's a teddy bear and a doll and a picture book. . . ."

Konrad interrupted her. "It's more sensible for a boy of seven to play with one thing at a time, isn't it? He ought to concentrate on it properly, and not annoy the grown-ups."

"I'm sorry . . . I never thought of that," stammered Mrs. Bartolotti. But she put all the toys she had bought down in Konrad's corner by the door, including the doll that could say MAMA. Konrad looked at the doll.

"Is that for me?" he asked, and when Mrs. Bartolotti nodded, he said, "But I'm a boy of seven!"

"Is a doll that says MAMA wrong for boys of seven?" asked Mrs. Bartolotti.

"Dolls are for *girls* of seven," Konrad told her. Mrs. Bartolotti picked up the doll from the floor.

"Oh, what a pity!" she murmured. "Such a pretty doll, too!"

Mrs. Bartolotti put the doll's bangs of golden hair straight, and patted her, and decided to give the doll to the little girl who lived in the apartment below hers. The little girl's name was Kitty.

Konrad was building a tall tower of blocks.

"Konrad . . ." said Mrs. Bartolotti. And she told him she really ought to do some work now.

Mrs. Bartolotti made the most beautiful, brightly colored rugs in the whole city. The dealers and furnishing stores that sold her rugs used to tell their customers, "Ah, Mrs. Bartolotti is a real artist! Her rugs are little masterpieces!"

"I must get at least two inches of rug made today," she said, and she asked Konrad if he minded being left alone in the room or if he'd rather go into her workroom with her. "So you'd have company," she said.

Konrad was busy building a second tall tower.

"That's all right," he said. "I'll stay here. I knew you might be a working mother. They told us most children's mothers have jobs these days. And there are some children who live with their grannies, and some children who spend the day with babysitters, and some who are door-key children."

"Heavens above!" whispered Mrs. Bartolotti to herself, feeling rather confused again. She went into her workroom, sat down at her frame, and worked threads of bright red, deep violet and lime green into the rug she was making, and quite forgot about the strange little boy she had left in a corner of the living room. When she was working, Mrs. Bartolotti never thought of anything but the rug she was making, which was why her rugs always turned out so beautiful.

Since Mrs. Bartolotti was thinking of nothing but the rug, she didn't notice how fast the time was passing either, but suddenly she saw Konrad standing beside her. Mrs. Bartolotti looked first at Konrad, then at her watch, and saw it was evening.

"Gracious, you really *must* be hungry by now!" she cried in dismay.

"Not really," said Konrad. He told her he'd really come to ask about something else. He wanted to sing a song, but he didn't know any songs for boys of seven; they'd left that out of the preparation process, he said. Or perhaps, he added, it *had* been part of the preparation process, but he hadn't been paying attention well enough at the time.

"Do tell me about this preparation process!" said Mrs. Bartolotti, full of curiosity. "What was it like? And who did it?"

Konrad did not reply.

"I mean, did you have special teachers, or was it done by factory workers? And were you crumpled up the whole time? I'm sorry, I mean—well, all dried up, like before you had the nutrient solution?"

Konrad still did not reply.

"Or would you rather not talk about it?"

"I'm only supposed to talk about it in an emergency," Konrad said. "Is this an emergency?"

"Oh no, it isn't an emergency!" said Mrs. Bartolotti. And she tried to remember the songs she had known as a child.

The first one she thought of was "A tisket, a tasket, a green and yellow basket . . ." But she couldn't get any further than that. Then she remembered "I've lost my underwear, I don't care, I'll go bare. Bye-bye, long johns" and "Oh, I stuck my head in the little skunk's hole," and "No matter how young a prune may be, he's always full of wrinkles."

Mrs. Bartolotti sang song after song, enjoying herself more all the time. She sang, "Nobody loves me, everybody hates me! Think I'll go eat worms." And she sang, "I had a little teddy bear, his name was Tiny Tim. I put him in the bathtub to see if he could swim. . . ." And as she sang, she noticed that Konrad was growing steadily paler and paler. However, she thought he'd like the rest of the rhyme because it was so funny, so she went on, "He drank all the water, he ate all the soap, he died the next morning with a bubble in his throat."

Konrad was deathly white now—white as a sheet. Mrs. Bartolotti couldn't help noticing. So, to cheer him up, she sang, "My eyes have seen the glory of the burning of the school. . . ."

Here Konrad started to cry.

"Konrad! What's the matter?" Mrs. Bartolotti jumped up, taking a tissue out of her jeans pocket, and wiped Konrad's face.

"I can't help crying!" Konrad sobbed. "I don't know what I ought to do! Boys of seven are supposed to listen hard when their mothers talk to them or tell them stories or sing to them. But boys of seven are supposed to stop listening at once whenever someone says something naughty or tells a naughty story or sings a naughty song!"

"Did I sing a naughty song?" Mrs. Bartolotti was horrified. Konrad nodded. So Mrs. Bartolotti promised him never to say or sing anything naughty again, and he stopped crying.

Then someone rang the bell. Not the way the mailman or the firemen would ring it, three quiet little rings in quick succession. Only Mr. Thomas the druggist rang the bell that way. It was Saturday, and he and Mrs. Bartolotti were friends on Saturday.

"Goodness me, I nearly forgot Tommy!" cried Mrs. Bartolotti, running to the door. She knocked her elbow against the cabinet in the hall and nearly said, "Damn!" but stopped herself just in time, in case Konrad felt he had to start crying again.

Chapter Three ─────────────

Mr. Thomas was wearing his black suit and his light gray tie, and carrying a bunch of violets.

"I've got two theater tickets," he said.

"I've got a little boy," said Mrs. Bartolotti.

"Second row, center aisle," said Mr. Thomas, and then he stopped short, stared at Mrs. Bartolotti and asked, "What? *What* did you say?"

At that moment Konrad himself came into the hall, went up to Mr. Thomas, shook hands and said, "Good evening, sir."

"This is my son!" said Mrs. Bartolotti. "He's seven years old, and his name is Konrad."

Mr. Thomas went pale. Even paler than Konrad listening to the naughty songs. Mrs. Bartolotti felt she owed Mr. Thomas an explanation, but she didn't want to explain in front of Konrad, so she said, "Konrad dear, I think there's a children's program on television."

"Oh, great!" said Konrad, obediently going off to the living room. Mrs. Bartolotti called after him, "Press the top knob first, and then the third button from the bottom, and then . . ."

"Yes, I know, thank you," Konrad called back from the living room. "They taught us how to watch television."

Mrs. Bartolotti took Mr. Thomas into the kitchen, gave him a cigar, lit one herself, put the water on for coffee and told Mr. Thomas the whole story. By the time the kettle boiled she had finished telling him, but Mr. Thomas still didn't believe her, even by the time all the water had finally trickled down through the coffee filter. He was not convinced until Mrs. Bartolotti showed him the empty can and the empty packet of nutrient solution and the documents and the letter.

"Awkward!" said Mr. Thomas. "Very awkward indeed!" Mrs. Bartolotti nodded in agreement. Mr. Thomas studied the toes of his shiny black patent leather shoes.

"Everybody sitting comfortably?" asked a voice on the children's television program in the living room. "Yes!" said Konrad, and "YES!" shouted at least a hundred children in the television studio. Mr. Thomas was still studying the toes of his patent leather shoes.

"Say something, Tommy," Mrs. Bartolotti said.

"Send him back," said Mr. Thomas, in a quiet voice.

"What a thing to say!" exclaimed Mrs. Bartolotti, in an even quieter voice. She took Mr. Thomas's hand, pulled him up from his chair and led him through the kitchen and the hall to the living room door.

"There! Look!" whispered Mrs. Bartolotti.

Mr. Thomas looked. He saw a plastic crocodile with green scales and a purple tail and two round red eyes on the television screen. The program was a Punch and Judy puppet show. The crocodile was creeping up behind Punch, who wore a pointed cap and had a wooden head and who didn't know that the crocodile was there.

And Mr. Thomas saw Konrad sitting in front of the

television set. Konrad was wearing his blue cap with the little golden bell, his eyes and his mouth were wide open and the forefinger of his right hand was resting on the tip of his nose. His ears were bright red, and the fair hair sticking out from under his cap was untidy. All in all, Konrad was the very image of a dear little boy in need of love and protection.

"Well?" whispered Mrs. Bartolotti.

"No," murmured Mr. Thomas, shaking his head sadly. "No, you can't send the little kid back!"

"You see?" said Mrs. Bartolotti.

On the television screen, Punch, who had turned out to have a fair idea of what was going on after all, was just killing the plastic crocodile, and the hundred or so children in the studio were screeching like monkeys. Konrad removed his forefinger from his nose and got up, saying, "Poor crocodile! Poor crocodile!" He went over to the television set and pushed the button. The picture on the screen disappeared even before the crocodile had turned all four scaly feet up in the air.

"Don't you like Punch and Judy shows?" asked Mr. Thomas. (As a child, Mr. Thomas himself had hated Punch and Judy shows.)

"We should be kind to poor dumb animals!" said Konrad.

"But it was a crocodile, Konrad!" cried Mrs. Bartolotti. "Crocodiles are nasty. They eat people up!"

"That crocodile only wanted to take a nap," said Konrad. "And the person in the red cap woke the poor thing up, shouting and yelling like that!"

"Oh, but the crocodile was creeping up behind him," said Mrs. Bartolotti (who had loved Punch and Judy shows as a child herself).

"I don't think animals know it's wrong to creep up behind someone," said Konrad.

"No, but . . ." stammered Mrs. Bartolotti.

"And anyway, that person in the red cap shouldn't be in a wildlife park unless he's driving through it in a car with all the windows closed," Konrad pointed out. "That would be much safer for him *and* the crocodile."

"Yes, but . . ." stammered Mrs. Bartolotti again.

"But nothing!" cried Mr. Thomas, sounding very pleased. "The boy's right! He's a remarkably bright boy for his age!" And Mr. Thomas looked at Konrad with great approval. Normally, Mr. Thomas never looked at children with great approval. Or even with moderate approval.

Mr. Thomas's approval became positive enthusiasm when Konrad asked, "Is it bedtime now, please?"

"Tired?" asked Mrs. Bartolotti.

"That doesn't matter," said Konrad. "Most children aren't tired when it's their bedtime."

Mrs. Bartolotti knew as little about children's bedtimes as she did about the right time to eat ice cream. All she could remember was the way she used to yell her head off as a child when she was sent to bed, and how she often used to lie awake talking to herself out loud.

"Never mind," she told Konrad. "Just stay up as long as you like. You'll soon know when you feel like bedtime." And as she said that she realized that the bed had not been delivered yet. "Anyway, that solves the bedtime question," she said. "You can go to bed when your bed arrives." Konrad thought that would be all right.

Konrad was still not hungry, even though Mrs. Bartolotti asked him, "Would you like a candy?"

"It's very, very bad for children to eat candies in the evening just before they go to bed," said Konrad.

All the same, Mrs. Bartolotti held a chocolate in front of his mouth, a strawberry cream with an almond on top. She held it there until Konrad opened his mouth, and then she popped the chocolate in.

"Bertie, dear, you have no sense at all!" Mr. Thomas scolded her. "That boy knows better than you! You ought to be glad to have a child who knows how bad sugar is for your teeth."

Mrs. Bartolotti muttered something that sounded like "baloney," and looked at Konrad to see how pleased he would look when he tasted the delicious chocolate. But he did not look pleased at all, far from it. He looked very unhappy. He choked the chocolate down, and then said, "Thank you, it was very good, but it makes me feel all upset!"

"Oh, come, Konrad!" said Mrs. Bartolotti, laughing. "One chocolate couldn't possibly upset you! You'd need to eat a whole bag of them!"

Konrad shook his head, explaining that the candy hadn't upset his stomach; it upset his feelings, because children aren't allowed to eat chocolates just before they go to bed, and, he said, doing things that were not allowed upset him. That was how he had been taught. And, Konrad added very sadly, up to now he'd always been proud of feeling so upset at the mere idea of doing things that were not allowed, because that was one of the most important subjects they were taught in the Final Preparation Department.

"It's called Guilt Feelings," Konrad said. "And Instant Children who haven't learned it properly aren't allowed to leave the factory." Then he looked frightened and stopped, remembering suddenly that he wasn't supposed to talk about the factory except in an emergency.

"How awful!" murmured Mrs. Bartolotti. Mr. Thomas, however, said, "This is the best boy I've ever met. If all children were like that I'd have had one myself long ago! It's a real joy to find such a well-mannered, good, polite little boy! Only seven, too!"

"Tommy, you're an idiot!" said Mrs. Bartolotti. But Mr. Thomas did not hear her, because he was still busy praising Konrad to the skies.

He went on and on about Konrad for quite some time, not even stopping for the delivery of the child's bed when it finally arrived. He was still talking as Mrs. Bartolotti put a pillow case on one of her sofa cushions, he was still talking as she made up Konrad's bed with a sheet, and he was still talking as she fluffed her best and softest comforter. He kept saying what a wonderfully well-mannered child Konrad was, how unusual it was to find such a boy, and how a child like that needed encouragement, more encouragement than Mrs. Bartolotti could offer him.

Mrs. Bartolotti nodded in agreement to all that (probably because she had stopped listening), and plumped up the pillow and straightened the comforter on the child's bed. However, when she caught the word *father* three times in quick succession in Mr. Thomas's long speech, she stopped nodding. She pushed the child's bed into the bedroom, called out, "Just a moment, Tommy," came back, sat down opposite Mr. Thomas in her rocking chair and asked, "Now then. What was that you were saying about a father, Tommy?"

"He needs one," said Mr. Thomas. "Badly."

"Well, he's got one!" said Mrs. Bartolotti. "It says so on his birth certificate! Konrad Augustus Bartolotti. That's his father!"

"If Konrad Augustus Bartolotti is his father," said Mr. Thomas, frowning so hard that four deep lines appeared on his forehead, "then he'd better come back and take a proper interest in the upbringing of this delightful child! It's his duty!"

At that point Mrs. Bartolotti lost her temper. She yelled that she had no need whatever of Konrad Augustus, and when Konrad Augustus had been living with her she'd wished him in Katmandu, which was apparently where he had gone, and she hoped to heaven he'd stay there.

"In that case someone must take the place of the boy's father, and I . . ." began Mr. Thomas. Then he had to stop, because Konrad appeared in the doorway of the living room, asking where he could wash and if there was a toothbrush for him.

There wasn't any toothbrush, but Mrs. Bartolotti took her jeans and T-shirts out of the sink so Konrad could wash. "Wait just a minute and I'll clean up the bathroom," she told Konrad. She was feeling very sorry for herself. Cleaning up was the kind of work she hated most of all.

When she came back into the living room she found Mr. Thomas and Konrad sitting side by side, smiling.

"I'm Konrad's father now!" said Mr. Thomas. "He says that's all right." Konrad nodded. Mrs. Bartolotti looked at Thomas, looked at Konrad, sighed and said, "Oh well, then, I suppose it *is* all right."

She did not really feel it was all right, not one little bit. For one thing, she didn't believe it was absolutely essential for a boy of seven to have a father. For another, she thought that if he *was* to have a father, why should it be such a boring old stick as Thomas? I'm fond enough of Thomas, she thought, he's a good sort of friend to see twice a week—but I don't see him being a father!

However, she repeated. "Well, that's fine!" because Konrad was smiling so happily.

Later, when Konrad was tucked in bed fast asleep—"like a little angel," as Mr. Thomas put it—Mr. Thomas and Mrs. Bartolotti were sitting in the living room. Mr. Thomas was drinking a small whiskey with a lot of soda in it, and Mrs. Bartolotti was drinking a large vodka with a cherry in it.

"You'll have to go and register Konrad for school tomorrow," said Mr. Thomas.

"Tomorrow is Sunday," said Mrs. Bartolotti. "Children don't go to school on Sundays."

"Well, you must take him to school the day after tomorrow, then," said Mr. Thomas. He added that he was already looking forward to Konrad getting an A in every subject. What a proud father he was going to be! Mrs. Bartolotti couldn't manage to feel like a particularly proud mother when she thought of Konrad's future grades.

She wanted to watch a movie on television, but Mr. Thomas stopped her, saying, "Never mind that rubbish! I want a serious word with you!" So Mrs. Bartolotti did not turn the television on; she listened to Mr. Thomas instead. He wanted not just one serious word, but about a hundred thousand, and when he finally stopped, it was after midnight. Mrs. Bartolotti yawned, said, "Good night, Tommy dear." After Mr. Thomas had left the apartment she went to bed very quietly, so as not to disturb Konrad. But though she was so tired she couldn't sleep, Mr. Thomas's serious words kept going through her head.

"You must alter radically! You must be neater and more maternal, and behave better!

"You must shape up! You can't keep wearing such peculiar clothes!

"You must see to it that you clean the apartment and cook proper meals, and you must be careful not to say anything except things that are fit for the ears of a boy of seven . . . things that will improve his mind!

"You must . . . you must . . . you must . . ."

By the time the list had gone through Mrs. Bartolotti's head some two thousand times, she had remembered all Mr. Thomas's serious words. She dropped off to sleep, but even in her sleep she groaned aloud, muttering, "You must . . . you must . . . you must . . ."

Chapter Four —————

The next morning Mrs. Bartolotti woke up much earlier than usual, rubbed her eyes and looked over at Konrad's bed. Konrad's bed was empty. Mrs. Bartolotti was alarmed; she jumped out of bed, thinking for a moment that Konrad was only a dream, and ran to the living-room door. There was Konrad sitting in his play corner. He had washed, and brushed his hair. He was building towers of blocks, murmuring, "These are units, and these are tens, and these are hundreds."

"What are you doing, Konrad?"

"I'm practicing arithmetic," said Konrad. "I'll be going to school tomorrow, so I thought I'd better get ready like a good boy."

"Like a good boy!" muttered Mrs. Bartolotti on her way to the kitchen, and when she was quite sure Konrad was out of earshot she added, "*Good!* I hate that word! It's as bad as *steady* or *neat* or *well-behaved!* Oh, rats!"

There were a lot of words Mrs. Bartolotti hated. In addition to *good* and *steady* and *neat* and *well-behaved,* she also hated *necessary, sensible, every day, proper, manners, usual, housewife,* and *correct.*

So Mrs. Bartolotti stood in her kitchen brewing coffee,

boiling eggs, making an omelet filled with strawberry jam especially for Konrad and thinking of those nasty, ugly words. She thought of Thomas's hundred thousand serious words too. She cleared the kitchen table, spread it with a green and pink flowered tablecloth, and took the plastic tea set for twenty-four out of the living-room closet. (Only one-twelfth of it, of course.) Since she had no flowers, she put a bunch of chives and a bunch of parsley in a glass of water in the middle of the kitchen table. Looking at the table, she thought, Well, even old Thomas would say that was all right! You can't get much neater, or more maternal, over getting breakfast than that!

Konrad drank his coffee and ate his omelet, and then a roll and butter, and then a roll and ham. "My goodness, you *are* hungry!" said Mrs. Bartolotti.

"Not especially," said Konrad. "I'm quite full now. . . . I don't think I'll be able to eat much more."

"Well, stop eating, then!"

"Oh, but you're supposed to eat up what's put on the table," Konrad told her. "And you always have to finish what's on your plate."

Mrs. Bartolotti swiftly picked up the last three rolls, the big slice of ham and the cheese, and put them all on the kitchen counter so there was nothing to eat left on the table. Konrad heaved a sigh of relief.

Usually Mrs. Bartolotti worked on Sundays, but that day she thought, I'm sure a boy of seven would like to get outdoors on Sunday, go for a walk, or play ball. Or perhaps Konrad would like to go to the playground, or the zoo!

But Konrad did not want to go out to the zoo or the playground or the park. He said, "I'd like to get ready for going to school tomorrow. I've learned to read and write and do arithmetic. We had a good course of preparation. But I don't know how far ahead with their work the children here will be." And he asked Mrs. Bartolotti if she would be very kind and go to see a child of seven and borrow the child's schoolbooks so he could look at them.

"But won't you be going into second grade, with the other children your age?" asked Mrs. Bartolotti. "I'm sure the others won't have got very far."

Konrad shook his head, and said no, he hoped he wouldn't have to go into second grade, because he wasn't just an Instant Child, he was a special child, considerably more intelligent than the average child, so it would be a pity if he didn't use his mental abilities to the full. He said he hoped to be put in third grade at least.

Mrs. Bartolotti sighed again. Then she went down to the second floor (her own apartment was on the third floor) and rang the doorbell of the apartment right below hers, where the Robertson family lived. Kitty Robertson was in third grade. Mr. Robertson opened the door. Kitty was standing right behind him staring at Mrs. Bartolotti, full of curiosity. Mrs. Robertson was standing behind Kitty, even fuller of curiosity. Although they had been living in the same building for over five years, Mrs. Bartolotti had never spoken to the Robertsons before. In fact, Mrs. Bartolotti did not often speak to any of the other people in the building, because they did not often want to speak to her. They said Mrs. Bartolotti was "peculiar," because of her odd clothes, and all the makeup she wore, and the way she used to talk to herself on the stairs.

Mrs. Bartolotti had no idea that the other people in the

building thought she was so peculiar, but when she saw th
three Robertsons staring at her so full of curiosity, it did
strike her that her request was going to sound rather odd.
Why would a grown woman want to borrow schoolbooks?

"Can we help you?" asked Mr. Robertson.

Mrs. Bartolotti's mind was in a whirl. She tried to think
up a good story. She thought of saying, My nephew has
come to stay and wants something to read. Or, I have to
make a rug and work something from a child's reader into
the pattern. Or, There's such a pretty picture on page
twenty-three of the third-grade arithmetic book.

"Can we help you?" asked Mr. Robertson again.

Mrs. Bartolotti decided all the stories she had invented
sounded silly, so she told the truth.

"Well, it's like this. My son is going to school tomorrow,
and he wants to have a look at the textbooks first, and
since your daughter is in third grade, I thought you might
be kind enough to lend him the books for a little while.
I'll bring them back later today."

Mr. and Mrs. Robertson were well mannered, and being
well-mannered people they did not ask a lot of questions,
though they looked very surprised and taken aback. However, they both said, "Yes, of course!"

Kitty Robertson was a well-mannered child, too, but
not, of course, so well-mannered as an adult yet. She had
only been around for a few years, so she had not had time
to learn about all the things a well-mannered person
doesn't do. "Oh, have you really got a son, Mrs. Bartolotti?" she asked.

"Ssh!" whispered Mrs. Robertson, adding, in an even
quieter whisper, "People don't ask questions like that!"

Kitty nodded and went into her room to get her reader and her arithmetic book. Mrs. Bartolotti took the two books, said, "Thank you," and went upstairs again. Mr. Robertson closed the door of their apartment.

"There, they weren't a bit surprised!" said Mrs. Bartolotti to herself, opening the door of her own apartment. "Anyway, why should they be? It's perfectly normal for a woman to have a son, after all."

If Mrs. Bartolotti could have seen through the floorboards she would have realized that she was wrong, since the Robertson family were evidently astonished to hear she had a son. All three of them were still standing on the other side of their front door, gaping at it, and murmuring, "A son! A son of seven! Well, I'll be . . . She has a son!"

Then Mrs. Robertson snorted. "If she has a son, I'll eat my hat!" she said.

"And even supposing she does have a son, where are his own books?" said Mr. Robertson. "If he's ready to go into third grade, why hasn't he started school before?"

"Can I go up later and see her son?" Kitty Robertson asked.

"Oh no, you can't just go like that without being invited!" said Mrs. Robertson.

"I could go ask for my books back," said Kitty.

"Yes, that's a possibility," said Mr. Robertson. "Not too early, though; that would look inquisitive. You can go late in the afternoon."

Kitty was very pleased. She could hardly wait for afternoon to come.

Konrad was delighted with the reader and the arithmetic book, though he was rather shocked to see all the little matchstick men and the flowers Kitty had drawn in the margins of the arithmetic book. And she had filled in all the capital Os in her reader with crayon. "Are school-children allowed to do that?" he asked. Mrs. Bartolotti wasn't sure if they were allowed to or not; they hadn't been allowed to in her own time, she said.

"But that was ages ago!" she added. "Perhaps everything's different in schools these days."

"That must be it," said Konrad.

Mrs. Bartolotti gave Konrad a pencil and a ball-point pen and some lined paper, and Konrad did arithmetic and looked through the books and read out loud, and read to himself, and wrote down words and sentences. Mrs. Bartolotti felt she wasn't needed at the moment, and decided to make the long fringes for the green rug. She was to have delivered the green rug two weeks earlier, but knotting fringes on rugs was very boring, so Mrs. Bartolotti used to put it off from day to day and then from week to week. She always put off boring work until she needed some money urgently. She needed money urgently now, because she had spent every penny she had on Konrad's clothes.

Mrs. Bartolotti took out a ball of green wool and a wooden board. She wound the wool around and around the wooden board, and then cut through all the threads with her big scissors so that she had a big bunch of woolen threads all the same length. "Now then, my dear, find the big crochet hook and pull the threads through the edge of the rug!" said Mrs. Bartolotti to herself.

"Yes, Mom!" said Konrad.

It took Mrs. Bartolotti some time to explain to Konrad

that when she said "my dear" out loud she didn't necessarily mean him, and just as he finally got the idea the doorbell rang. Konrad went to open the door, and came back with Mr. Thomas.

"Good gracious me!" said Mrs. Bartolotti. "What are you doing here?"

"What?" said Mr. Thomas. "I hope I'm not intruding?"

"No, of course not," said Mrs. Bartolotti, "but Saturday was yesterday, and it won't be Tuesday till the day after tomorrow."

"That doesn't matter now that I'm Konrad's father," explained Mr. Thomas.

"Konrad's father . . . so you are," muttered Mrs. Bartolotti. She cleared her throat. "Er—how often do fathers come visiting?" she asked.

"As often as they can," said Mr. Thomas.

Mrs. Bartolotti was thinking that though Mr. Thomas worked eight hours a day in his drugstore, he didn't have anything else to do. He had no wife or friends, he didn't have any children (apart from Konrad), he didn't play tennis or go to ball games or read books or watch television, he didn't go for long walks and he didn't play chess.

"I suppose you'll be coming to visit quite a bit," said Mrs. Bartolotti. She didn't sound too happy.

"Yes, of course," cried Mr. Thomas. *He* sounded delighted. "Konrad and I will be spending every spare moment we can together. Except when he's asleep, of course. He won't be needing his father when he's asleep."

Mrs. Bartolotti pulled tassel after tassel of her fringe through the thick edge of the rug, earnestly hoping that

Konrad slept well, soundly, and for a very long time every day.

Then Mr. Thomas tested Konrad on his arithmetic. Not just the exercises on the first page, but the difficult ones toward the end of the book too. Konrad could do it all, and he generally had the right answers worked out even before Mr. Thomas did. Konrad could read as well as an adult, and he could write beautifully too.

"This child shouldn't be in second grade or third grade either!" cried Mr. Thomas, enthusiastically. "He ought to go into fourth grade or fifth grade!"

"Boys of seven can't possibly go into fifth grade!" said Mrs. Bartolotti, tugging grimly at a thread of wool that refused to go through the edge of the rug.

"They can if they're as clever as my Konrad!"

Mrs. Bartolotti let go of the thread of wool. "Your Konrad? What do you mean, your Konrad?"

"I'm sorry. I meant our Konrad."

"Well, I mean *my* Konrad," said Mrs. Bartolotti, rather tartly.

"Let's not quarrel about it—certainly not in front of the child, Bertie dear," said Mr. Thomas. Mrs. Bartolotti nodded, picked up the piece of wool again and tugged at it. "All the same, a boy of seven can't go into fifth grade, however smart he is! They wouldn't let him."

"Then he must have a special tutor! Surely some kind of provision must be made for especially gifted children!"

"Please, I don't want any special tutor," said Konrad. "I'm sure it wouldn't be right! I know I'll fit into third grade. Children don't just learn reading and writing and arithmetic in school. They also learn to be part of a community, and they learn singing and drawing and physical education. I haven't done any of that yet, and I'd like to do those things."

"Very well, then, if that's how you feel," said Mr. Thomas.

Konrad had found several things in the reader that he didn't understand. He didn't know what geraniums were, or who Santa Claus was, and he didn't know what roses and carnations were either, and he had never heard of a church.

First Mr. Thomas gave him a little talk about Santa Claus. Konrad listened carefully, and when Mr. Thomas had finished his talk, he looked at a piece of paper where he had been making notes. "Thank you," said Konrad. "Shall I repeat it to you now? Santa Claus has a sleigh with reindeer, and he comes down from the sky at Christmastime to give children presents. Rich children get lots of presents, poorer children don't get so many presents, and very poor children don't get any presents. But Santa Claus is giving things to the ones who do get presents because it is Baby Jesus's birthday. Did I get it right?"

Mrs. Bartolotti giggled. Mr. Thomas stammered, "Er . . . well, Konrad, I don't know that that was quite the . . . listen, Konrad . . ."

"Oh, do be quiet, Tommy!" Mrs. Bartolotti interrupted. She told Konrad, "None of that is true. There isn't any Santa Claus! There aren't any fairies either."

"Any what?" asked Konrad.

"Fairies!" said Mrs. Bartolotti. "They're all stories parents and grandparents and aunts and uncles have made up to tell children."

"Why?"

Mrs. Bartolotti shrugged her shoulders. "How should I know? I suppose adults like to think they can trick children into believing things. It makes them feel good and clever. . . ."

"Bertie, dear, please . . ." Mr. Thomas tried to interrupt her.

"You just let me finish!" said Mrs. Bartolotti. "Because the things I'm telling Konrad *are* true! Adults are always trying to take children in. What they're really doing is saying, Just look at us, aren't we strong and clever and wonderful and good. . . ."

"Please, Bertie, I beg you! That is no way to talk in front of a child!" whispered Mr. Thomas. "Pull yourself together, Bertie!"

"Truth is truth!" snapped Mrs. Bartolotti. "And that goes for children too!"

"Come now, Bertie, do calm down!" Mr. Thomas implored her.

"You," snapped Mrs. Bartolotti, "are getting on my nerves!" Mr. Thomas sighed, and then he decided to take Konrad for a walk. "We'll go and look at a church first," he said. "And then we'll find a florist and see if there are roses and carnations and geraniums in the window. Get your cap, Konrad, and we'll go out. Your mother isn't in a very good mood today."

Konrad went for his cap. "I'm ready, Dad," he said. "Good-bye, Mom." And he and Mr. Thomas went out.

Watching them go, Mrs. Bartolotti made a face—a really horrible face. When the door of the apartment had closed behind them, she said to herself, "Having a child is all very well, I've nothing against that. It's having a father about the place that's getting me down. I'm sure I never needed one of *them!* I didn't order one, either!"

Not much else happened that day. Kitty Robertson came to get her schoolbooks, and was very disappointed to hear that Mrs. Bartolotti's son had gone for a walk with his father. She stayed with Mrs. Bartolotti for over half an hour, thinking, Perhaps he will be back soon. After she had been sitting in the living room with Mrs. Bartolotti for over half an hour, looking at Konrad's picture book and reading the story, and fixing the doll's beautiful golden hair, there was another ring at the door of the apartment. This time it was Mrs. Robertson.

"I'm so sorry my daughter has been bothering you for such a long time," she said in a very polite, sugary voice. "We only said she could come to fetch her books!" Then she turned to Kitty. "Come along now, supper's getting cold," she said in a very nasty voice. "People shouldn't stay so long when they haven't been invited."

Mrs. Bartolotti assured her that anyone was welcome to stay in her apartment as long as they liked, even if they hadn't been invited.

"Oh no, it was very bad manners!" said Mrs. Robertson, using her sugary voice again. Mrs. Bartolotti wanted to give Kitty the golden-haired doll, but Mrs. Robertson said she couldn't possibly accept such an expensive present. "Certainly not!" she snapped at Kitty, who was just putting out her hand for the doll.

"But we don't need a doll here," said Mrs. Bartolotti.

"Oh, please, Mom! Please, please, please!" cried Kitty.

"No, really!" said Mrs. Robertson. "I really couldn't accept something like that, I couldn't possibly!"

They went on like this about five times more, until finally Mrs. Bartolotti's patience was exhausted, and she said, "No one wants you to accept anything! I'm giving the doll to your daughter, and *she* wants it!"

"Oh yes! Oh yes, I do!" cried Kitty, seizing the doll. She clasped it so tight that Mrs. Robertson could see she wasn't going to let go of it without a struggle. "Well then, say thank you, Kitty!" she said in her nice, sugary voice.

Kitty said "Thank you," and Mrs. Robertson took her arm and pushed her out the door. As she was leaving, Mrs. Robertson said, "You really shouldn't have!" three more times.

Mrs. Bartolotti shut the door of the apartment, thinking how complicated people were and how very, very tiring. Then an idea struck her: She ought to cook supper, and she had nothing at all in the place to cook. Then another idea struck her: They could go out and have *steak au poivre* and mushrooms and French fried potatoes. Then a third idea struck her: They couldn't, because there was no money left in her change purse or her wallet or her little leather bag or her plastic folder. Mrs. Bartolotti was quite used to this state of affairs, and she didn't mind going without supper once in a while herself. But she remembered all Thomas's serious words. "My dear," she told herself, "a good mother would have a hot supper waiting for her little boy."

Mrs. Bartolotti sat down in her rocking chair in the living room and waited for something to occur to her. What occurred to her was this.

Dear old Tommy would insist on being a father. Very well, so now he's Konrad's father. And a father is supposed to pay for his son! Child support, that's what they call it.

So Tommy will have to pay me child support. In fact he'll have to pay me some child support this evening, and then I shall have some money, and we can go out for supper!

When Mr. Thomas and Konrad came back from their walk she told Mr. Thomas about it at once. He gave her a funny look, and then he said, stammering a bit, that he hadn't been prepared for this and he didn't have much money on him.

"Well, give me a deposit, then!" said Mrs. Bartolotti. So Mr. Thomas produced twenty dollars, and Mrs. Bartolotti was perfectly happy, because now they could have two steaks with mushrooms and French fries and raspberry sherbet to follow and apple juice to drink.

Then Mrs. Bartolotti and Konrad went out to the steak house, and Mr. Thomas went home.

When they got back to the apartment Konrad went to bed right away. Mrs. Bartolotti stayed up to knot another two feet of fringe along the edge of the green rug. "So as to have some money in the place tomorrow," she said to herself.

Apart from this, nothing else happened that Sunday. But to make up for it, a great many things happened the next day, which was Monday.

Chapter Five ─────────

Mrs. Bartolotti woke up at half past four the next morning. It was the first time in her life she had ever waked up so early. She climbed out of bed quietly, to avoid waking Konrad, but Konrad was already awake.

"I can't sleep anymore!" he said. "I'm so excited about going to school!"

Mrs. Bartolotti went into the bathroom. She looked at herself in the mirror and realized that this was one of her bad days. "Old as the hills, ugly as sin!" she informed her reflection. And she thought, When I take Konrad to school they'll never believe I'm his mother. They'll think I'm his grandmother. Or his great-grandmother!

At breakfast Mrs. Bartolotti's hands were trembling so badly that she broke an eggcup and a coffee cup.

"What's the matter?" asked Konrad. "Do people act the way you're acting now if they're nervous?"

Yes, and she *was* nervous, Mrs. Bartolotti admitted. She didn't know just how she was going to explain to the teachers that though Konrad was seven he'd never been to school before, and all the same he wanted to be in third grade.

"Fourth grade," said Konrad. "I was thinking about it

last night. I don't think third grade is the right class for me. The work would be too boring."

"But surely you'd need a report from another school, saying you'd done the third-year work before they let you into fourth grade!"

Konrad went to the kitchen drawer and took out the blue plastic envelope that contained his documents. There was a side pocket that Mrs. Bartolotti had missed. Konrad took a piece of stiff, light green paper out of this side pocket.

"Here it is!" he said.

"A report card? But which grade does it say you've been in?"

"I have to fill in the grade myself," Konrad told Mrs. Bartolotti, handing her the report.

It was headed ANNUAL REPORT in big black letters. Underneath was his name, *Konrad Bartolotti*. And under that were all the subjects, with V.G. for Very Good beside each of them. Konrad was Very Good in physical education, singing, drawing, conduct, reading, writing, arithmetic, science and English.

There was a piece on the back of the pale green report saying: *This pupil, Konrad Bartolotti, is ready to go into Grade————*.

And underneath was a signature, which was very difficult to read, but which looked something like "Hunbert" or "Honbert" or "Monbert."

There was a rubber-stamp mark above the signature. You couldn't read that, either.

"What school gave the report, though?" asked Mrs. Bartolotti. She turned the pale green report over, and now she saw that there was another line, also printed in very large letters, above the words ANNUAL REPORT. It said:

THE PRIMARY SCHOOL OF ZAIRE (CONGO).
RECOGNIZED BY THE DEPARTMENT
OF EDUCATION

"Oh, marvelous!" whispered Mrs. Bartolotti.

"Why? Because of all those Very Goods?" asked Konrad.

"But you've never been to the Congo, have you?" asked Mrs. Bartolotti.

"I'm afraid not," said Konrad. "But don't worry, the report is all right. You see, the Educational Department in the factory was a branch of the school in Zaire, so it's all aboveboard." Konrad cleared his throat, and went on, "And the children at that school all start when they're four, so it will be quite all right for me to go into fourth grade even though I am so young."

Mrs. Bartolotti was not quite convinced that everything really was all right, but it was nice to know she could produce a report card at the school, even if she was not perfectly easy in her own mind. "But suppose they ask you questions about this school in Zaire?" she said. "What will you say?"

Konrad said he thought he was probably better informed about Zaire than the average grade-school teacher; he'd been given a special briefing on the subject.

"All right, let's start off, then," said Mrs. Bartolotti.

She stuffed Konrad's birth certificate and inoculation records and the report card into her pocketbook, and put her fur hat and coat on.

"Wait a minute, Mom," said Konrad. "I need the report

card back." Mrs. Bartolotti dug the report out of her pocket-book. "And a ball-point pen," said Konrad. Mrs. Barto-lotti lent him a pen. Konrad wrote *Four* on the line on the back of the report, after the word *Grade*. So now it said: *This pupil, Konrad Bartolotti, is ready to go into Grade Four.*

Konrad gave the report card back to Mrs. Bartolotti, who put it in her pocketbook. Konrad put on his blue cap with the little bell and his patchwork jacket.

Kitty Robertson came running downstairs just behind them. She caught up when they were nearly at the bottom. She had a schoolbag on her back, and she looked at Konrad curiously.

"Hello. Are you going to be in third grade like me?" she asked.

Konrad shook his head. "No, I've been thinking it over," he said. "I have decided to be in fourth grade."

This reply surprised Kitty Robertson so much that she stopped on the stairs, rooted to the spot, staring at Konrad and Mrs. Bartolotti until they had disappeared from sight.

The way to the school led down the narrow street where Mrs. Bartolotti lived, into Main Street, and then you turned into another street seven blocks farther on and then into another narrow street where the school was.

As Konrad and Mrs. Bartolotti were walking along Main Street, Mrs. Bartolotti said, "You know, Konrad, I don't think it was a terribly good idea to tell Kitty Robert-son you'd been th—"

"I know," Konrad interrupted. "I realized that too. I won't be so careless the next time."

And as they turned into the narrow street where the school was, Konrad said, "You know, Mom, I don't really like having to be so . . . so . . ." He was searching for the right word, and found it just as they reached the school gates. "So careful of what I say," he finished. "I'd far rather tell everyone the truth, but as the head of the Final Preparation Department used to tell us, desperate situations call for desperate remedies, and, similarly, unusual situations call for unusual remedies."

"Quite right too, I'm sure," said Mrs. Bartolotti.

"And there's no denying I *am* an unusual situation," said Konrad. "I mean, in that most children come into the world in a different way. So I would surmise that unusual remedies are called for!"

"Absolutely right!" said Mrs. Bartolotti, opening the school gates. "Quite correct. But . . . now, Konrad, please don't take offense, but there's one more unusual remedy I think you might try. I think maybe you should talk more like an ordinary child when you're speaking to the teachers in this school."

"Don't I talk like an ordinary child? How do ordinary children talk?" asked Konrad.

"Well, I'm not too sure. I don't know very many seven year olds," said Mrs. Bartolotti, as they panted their way up the stairs to the second floor. "But I rather think seven-year-old children talk in a simpler way. . . . I mean, they don't know as many words as you do."

"Which words don't they know?"

But Mrs. Bartolotti had no chance to answer, because they had reached a door saying PRINCIPAL.

And Mr. Thomas the druggist was waiting by the door,

in his black suit, with a black tie, and a black briefcase under his arm.

"Hello, Tommy, what are you doing here?" asked Mrs. Bartolotti.

Mr. Thomas went "Ssh!" and motioned to Mrs. Bartolotti to speak more quietly. Then he whispered, "After all, I'm the boy's father. You may well need me if you encounter any problems, and of course I must stand by you both!"

Mrs. Bartolotti sighed, so loudly that Mr. Thomas went "Ssh!" again.

"Thomas, please!" she hissed at Mr. Thomas under her breath. "Go home—go to the drugstore—go anywhere you like, but go *away!*"

"Certainly not!" Mr. Thomas hissed back. "I'm the boy's father, and I'm staying!"

And he knocked on the door. A woman's voice said, "Come in!" Mr. Thomas opened the door and went into the principal's office, with Konrad and Mrs. Bartolotti close behind. Konrad took hold of Mrs. Bartolotti's hand.

"Yes?" said an elderly, plumpish lady. She was standing in front of her desk, holding a pile of workbooks.

"We want our son to come to this school," said Mr. Thomas.

The elderly, plumpish lady put the pile of workbooks down on the desk. "What—now? He'd be going into second grade, I suppose? But you should have registered him in the spring! The semester has started now, and it's one minute to nine already, and what's more, one of our teachers, Mrs. Stone, is out sick, and I have to take her place teaching 4A, and the bell will be ringing any moment!"

"No, we want him to go into third grade, not second grade, please," said Mr. Thomas.

"Er . . . no, fourth grade!" said Mrs. Bartolotti, casting an imploring glance at Mr. Thomas. "Fourth grade! He's already done the third-year work." She cast Mr. Thomas another, even more imploring glance. "In Zaire—Zaire! He did the third-year work in the Primary School of Zaire!"

Mr. Thomas had no idea what Mrs. Bartolotti was going on about, but he did get the message that he was to keep his mouth shut. The school bell rang, and the principal looked very anxious. "Oh dear, whatever am I to do with you?" she asked. "I can't leave 4A on their own for long—they're awful kids! I'll have to go."

Mrs. Bartolotti said surely it couldn't take very long to put a boy's name down for fourth grade. The principal said, well, there were a great many forms that had to be completed in great detail. However, she did sit down at her desk and asked Mrs. Bartolotti for Konrad's birth certificate, inoculation records and his last report card. Mr. Thomas stared, fascinated, at the report from the "Primary School of Zaire." The principal stared at it, fascinated, too. She was delighted to find she had acquired such a good pupil, from a school that was so far away, and she said. "Oh, no, it won't take long. I see you have the necessary papers with you. We get all kinds of difficulties when people leave them at home."

And the principal took Konrad straight off to 4A with her. She even lent him a pencil and a ball-point pen and a workbook, since he had no pens or pencils with him.

Mrs. Bartolotti and Mr. Thomas watched Konrad go up to the third floor with the principal. Mrs. Bartolotti was relieved that they had got him into the school without any trouble. However, Mr. Thomas was moaning quietly to himself; the big toe of his left foot was hurting him. That was because Mrs. Bartolotti had stamped on his foot three times while they were in the principal's room. She had done it on purpose; she did it whenever the principal had called Mr. Thomas "Mr. Bartolotti," and Mr. Thomas had opened his mouth to say, "Oh, but my name isn't Bartolotti." Mrs. Bartolotti had stamped on his foot when he got as far as "Oh, but . . . ," and Mr. Thomas had closed his mouth again.

"It wasn't very nice of you to stamp on my foot like that!" said Mr. Thomas now, as they went downstairs.

"Well, I'm sorry, but I had to," said Mrs. Bartolotti. In actual fact she was not at all sorry. She would happily have stamped on Mr. Thomas's foot once more for luck; she felt he was interfering with her life and Konrad's life far too much.

Mr. Thomas was offended, and walked away fast, in the direction of the drugstore, limping. And with any luck he's so offended we won't be seeing any more of *him* today! thought Mrs. Bartolotti grimly. There, however, she was wrong.

At exactly twelve-thirty Mrs. Bartolotti went to school to meet Konrad. There was Mr. Thomas, standing outside the school gates. He was still feeling offended, and he told Mrs. Bartolotti that he had had no way, after all, of knowing that she would be meeting Konrad. "You're usually so late for everything," he said.

That made Mrs. Bartolotti furious, because she was hardly ever late for anything; if it was important, Mrs.

Bartolotti was always on time. "Oh, you!" she cried. "People like you are always finding fault! Just because a person makes rugs for a living and doesn't have a husband and wears a lot of makeup, you think she's bound to be late! I ask you!"

"Hush—do please hush! People are staring," said Mr. Thomas. Then he took a couple of bills out of his pocket. "Here, that's the rest of the child support," he said. "I'll have some more for you on the first of next month."

Mrs. Bartolotti took the money and tried to smile, though she did not find it easy. The bell rung inside the building. "He'll be out in a minute," said Mr. Thomas. "I do hope he had a nice time!" said Mrs. Bartolotti. "I'm sure he'll have got an A on his very first day!" said Mr. Thomas. "I don't care about *that*," said Mrs. Bartolotti.

First a crowd of boys came out of school, then a crowd of girls, then some boys and girls together, and then Konrad.

Konrad saw Mrs. Bartolotti and Mr. Thomas and went over to them. Someone shouted out behind him, "Dummy Bartolotti, Dummy Bartolotti!" but Konrad did not turn around.

"Was it nice?" asked Mrs. Bartolotti.

"Did you get A's?" asked Mr. Thomas.

Konrad shook his head.

"No? Why not?" Mr. Thomas was disappointed. "Would you rather be in third grade after all?" he asked.

"Not on your life!" said Konrad. "Anyway it's all a lot of garbage, what they learn! And I didn't get a crummy A because I haven't finished a dumb assignment yet."

"Konrad, whatever are you saying?" Mr. Thomas was so surprised that he had seven frown lines on his forehead.

"I'm talking like an ordinary child," said Konrad. "Like the others." He turned to Mrs. Bartolotti. "I think I see what you meant this morning. I can *almost* do it now." And he turned to Mr. Thomas. "I didn't say anything in class today because I had to learn the right way to talk first. But tomorrow," said Konrad, smiling at Mr. Thomas, "tomorrow I'll raise my hand and answer questions, and if I finish an assignment I can get 100, if that's what you'd like."

They walked along Main Street together, with Konrad in between Mr. Thomas and Mrs. Bartolotti. "The only thing is," he said, "it's very difficult to be sure what's talking like an ordinary child and what's being rude. I'll have to do some more work on it."

As they turned into the street where Mrs. Bartolotti lived they saw Kitty Robertson walking along behind them. She waved to Konrad. Mrs. Bartolotti stopped.

"Isn't that the naughty little girl who lives in the apartment below you?" asked Mr. Thomas, and when Mrs. Bartolotti nodded, he said, "I don't want Konrad playing with that child! She's stuck out her tongue at me, several times!"

All of a sudden Mrs. Bartolotti felt she liked Kitty Robertson much better than ever before. "I shall be very happy for my son to play with Kitty!" she said.

"Well, I won't have *my* son playing with her!" said Mr. Thomas.

Kitty Robertson had almost caught up with them by

now. "Please, am I to play with her or not?" asked Konrad. "What do I do?"

"You're . . ." Mr. Thomas began, but then he yelled, "Yow!" because Mrs. Bartolotti had stamped on his foot once again.

"There you are!" Mrs. Bartolotti told Konrad, with a broad smile. "Your father says yes!"

Kitty had caught up with Konrad now. "Hello, Mrs. Bartolotti," she said, nodding to Mr. Thomas and smiling at Konrad. "It's my birthday today," Kitty went on. "And after school I'm having a party. Would you like to come? It starts at four o'clock. See you at four, okay?"

And Kitty Robertson ran on down the road. Probably she was in a hurry because of all the things she had to do for her party. Konrad walked slowly along the street with his parents.

"I am not in favor of this!" said Mr. Thomas. "She is a rude child!"

"Don't talk such nonsense!" cried Mrs. Bartolotti. "She's a perfectly ordinary child. And pretty, too!"

"Do you want to go *very* much?" Mr. Thomas asked Konrad.

Konrad thought about it, and then said he wasn't quite sure if he wanted to go to the party *very* much or not, but he did like Kitty Robertson. And it would be useful for him to go to Kitty's party, Konrad added, because he could learn some more real child language.

Mr. Thomas sighed. He didn't really want to forbid Konrad to do something he wanted to do, and besides, he was scared for his toes. Mrs. Bartolotti was looking at him in a very angry, fierce way. "It's quite simple, Konrad," she said. "When you go to Kitty's party this afternoon you're *my* son, and when you're lying quiet in bed at night then you're *his* son."

"Yes, Mom," said Konrad.

However, Mr. Thomas was not giving up yet. When they reached the door of the apartment building, he said he had just remembered that Konrad really ought to go to the playground that afternoon. "Thomas, will you kindly go back to your store!" cried Mrs. Bartolotti, shaking with rage.

Mr. Thomas did not much want to go back to the drugstore, which was closed for lunch anyway, and would not be opening again until two. That was still an hour away, and Mr. Thomas had intended to spend the hour in Mrs. Bartolotti's apartment. But Mrs. Bartolotti firmly squashed that idea. "We've got a lot to do," she said. "We have to find a birthday present for Kitty," she added, "and there isn't enough food for you, and we want to be alone, understand?"

Mr. Thomas said, "Well, good-bye then," and went off in the direction of the drugstore, looking sad. Konrad watched him go, and he looked sad too. "I feel sorry for Dad," Konrad said quietly.

"No need to feel sorry for *him*," said Mrs. Bartolotti, leading Konrad into the building. "Silly old so-and-so!"

"But he is my father, and I do like him!" By now Konrad was looking very sad indeed, and Mrs. Bartolotti hastened to assure him that she too liked Mr. Thomas very much indeed. Konrad looked happier.

After school, while Mrs. Bartolotti was looking for a birthday present for Kitty (she found a doll's tea set,

63

which she had once ordered, at the back of a closet in the living room), she realized that Konrad wanted to talk about Mr. Thomas.

He said, "Parents should get along well together. It's better for the children. When parents quarrel there's usually some right and some wrong on both sides. Human beings are all different, and we ought to put up with other people's little quirks."

Mrs. Bartolotti, washing the dusty doll's tea set, murmured, "Yes, dear," and "That's right." And she thought, I won't say another word about Thomas just now, because if I do I'll get angry and call him names, and that will make poor Konrad unhappy again. She also made a good resolution never to say anything nasty to Mr. Thomas again—at least, not in front of Konrad—and only to stamp on his feet when she was quite sure Konrad wasn't looking.

Chapter Six

At five minutes to four Konrad was standing in the hall of the apartment, all ready for the party. He had washed his face three times, brushed his hair twice, and polished his shoes. He was holding a shoe box wrapped in pink tissue paper, with a bow made of twelve loops of green ribbon on top. Mrs. Bartolotti had painted tiny red hearts all over the pink tissue paper. The doll's tea set was inside the box.

"You can go down now, Konrad," said Mrs. Bartolotti.

"But it isn't quite four o'clock yet." Konrad hesitated.

"A couple of minutes one way or the other doesn't matter," said Mrs. Bartolotti. But Konrad still hesitated. They heard footsteps and laughter—children's laughter—on the stairway outside.

"There, that's the other guests arriving," said Mrs. Bartolotti. Konrad nodded, but he still did not move. "She's invited Frank too," he said.

"Is Frank a nice boy?" asked Mrs. Bartolotti.

"He's the one who was shouting Dummy Bartolotti at me. That big fat boy."

"I'm sure he was only joking." Mrs. Bartolotti smiled to make it sound more convincing; she didn't want Konrad's feelings to be hurt.

"You really think so?" asked Konrad. He looked at the smiling Mrs. Bartolotti so hard that she stopped smiling, and shook her head sadly.

"Then why did you say so if you didn't think so?"

"I didn't want you to feel hurt."

"I don't see how telling me lies could stop me from feeling hurt," said Konrad. Then he asked why some children tease other children for no real reason. "They didn't tell us about that in the factory," Konrad said. "Can you tell me why?" But Mrs. Bartolotti couldn't, or at least not right away, though she promised to think about it and tell Konrad after the birthday party.

"And you'll tell me the truth?" asked Konrad.

"I promise I will," said Mrs. Bartolotti again.

"I'll go down now, then," said Konrad. Mrs. Bartolotti opened the door and watched Konrad go. When he reached the top of the stairs she called after him, "And if that great lump Frank calls you any more silly names, just wallop him!"

"Wallop him?" Konrad stopped. "What's that?"

Mrs. Bartolotti leaned out the doorway and called, "I mean hit him! Wallop him! Punch him! Knock his head off!"

Konrad shook his head. "They didn't teach me that either," he said. Then he went downstairs. Mrs. Bartolotti could not see him anymore, but she heard him ring the Robertsons' bell, and directly afterward she heard Kitty Robertson's voice saying, "Hi, Konrad. It's great you could come! Come in! Oh, what a pretty package! I bet that's going to be my nicest present."

Then Mrs. Bartolotti heard the door close. She shut her

own door, went into the bathroom and put on some fresh makeup, plenty of blue eye shadow, red lipstick and pink blusher. Then she went into her workroom, sat down at her frame and went on with the rug. She did a red flower with pink spots, on a blue background. The flower was not quite as beautiful as usual, because Mrs. Bartolotti was not thinking about it; she was thinking about children who tease other children. At first she thought it would be easy to explain, that they were just nasty, mean little horrors, and they were born that way. But then Mrs. Bartolotti remembered how her own mother was always saying, "Why can't you be more like your cousin Louise, honey? She's much, much better behaved than you are!" Bertie Bartolotti, as a child, had not liked hearing that, and whenever she met her cousin Louise, she used to stick out her tongue and yell "Yaaaah!" And Mrs. Bartolotti also remembered calling a little boy named Richard who lived next door "Pimple-Face." Now why did I do that? Mrs. Bartolotti wondered. I don't think I was a particularly nasty, mean little horror of a child. I expect I was glad I didn't have any pimples myself, thought Mrs. Bartolotti. And then she sighed, because she could see it was not so simple as she'd thought to decide why some children tease others, and it was going to be very difficult to explain it all to Konrad.

Meanwhile, Konrad was drinking hot chocolate in Kitty Robertson's playroom. There was also apple juice to drink and hot dogs and birthday cake to eat. A big striped lantern hung over the table. There were four other children there as well as Konrad and Kitty: Frank, Tony, Suzie and Carol. Frank and Suzie were in 4A, Tony and

Carol were in third grade, like Kitty. Frank was a whole head taller than Konrad, who was sitting next to him. So far he had not called Konrad "Dummy Bartolotti" once, and Konrad was relieved. Suzie and Carol were being nice to him, though they were nosey, and kept asking why he had only just come to live with Mrs. Bartolotti, and how could Mr. Thomas the druggist be his father when Mr. Thomas wasn't married to Mrs. Bartolotti? Konrad did not know what to say, and he was glad that Kitty kept interrupting all those questions, saying, "Leave him alone, will you!"

Tony was not nice to Konrad. He made faces at him and kicked him under the table. Tony was being mean to Konrad just because Kitty was being so nice to him; Tony wanted Kitty to be his girl friend, so he was jealous, though of course Konrad did not know that. Konrad had no idea what jealousy was anyway.

Then Tony knocked Konrad's cup of hot chocolate with his elbow as he reached for a piece of cake from the big plate in the middle of the table. The cup tipped over, and the chocolate flowed across the pink tablecloth to the very edge of the table, and dripped down onto the white rug.

"Oh, Mom—quick, the chocolate!" cried Kitty in horror. She knew how fond her mother was of that white rug; it was Mrs. Robertson's pride and joy.

Mrs. Robertson came running in with a wet cloth, and dabbed and rubbed at the chocolate stain, wailing, "For goodness' sake, can't you children be more careful? It's not as if you were still babies!" The chocolate stain would not go away.

69

"Wasn't me, wasn't me!" shouted Tony. "It was him, it was him!" He pointed at Konrad.

"Don't be so rotten!" cried Kitty. "Tony's telling lies."

"Oh, for heaven's sake stop quarreling!" snorted Mrs. Robertson. She kept rubbing and dabbing away like mad, and gradually she stopped looking quite so angry, because the chocolate stain was coming out. "You go into the living room; I must let this patch dry off. And you'll have more room in there. You can play sack races and egg and spoon races, but mind you only use the hard-boiled eggs. They're on the kitchen table."

The children went into the living room, and pushed the table and chairs into a corner. That left them plenty of room for sack races, egg and spoon races, and water-carrying competitions. Konrad had never played any of those games before, but he was very good at them. He got to the bedroom door first in the sack race, and he was the only one who managed to get his hard-boiled egg to the kitchen door without dropping it. He was also the only one who could carry a brimming glass of water to the bathroom door without spilling any. Frank dropped his egg right at the start, spilled half the glass of water before he reached the bathroom door, and came in last in the sack race. That made him very angry, and he started shouting "Dummy Bartolotti!" again. Tony shouted it too. "Dummy Bartolotti! Dummy Bartolotti!"

"Stop it this minute!" shouted Kitty. "Or I'll throw you out!"

Tony and Frank stopped, but they looked daggers at Konrad.

Kitty had been given a quiz game for her birthday, and

she wanted to play it. She got out the quiz game cards and the instructions, and Tony and Frank looked at them. "What stupid questions!" said Frank. "What a dumb game," said Tony. "We're not playing!" they both said. This was because they didn't know any of the answers to the questions, and when Konrad looked at the cards and said they weren't stupid questions at all, they just nudged each other and laughed at him. So Konrad started telling them the answers. "This one asks you what the capital of Poland is, and the answer's Warsaw," he said. "And the Leaning Tower is in Pisa, and the square root of a hundred and forty-four is twelve."

"Yah, yah, yah! Stupid little show-off!" shouted Tony.

"He's just making it up. Stupid little show-off. I'll show him!" shouted Frank, punching Konrad in the stomach.

"Go on, hit him!" Suzie whispered to Konrad. Konrad shook his head.

"He's yellow, he's too scared, yah, yaaah!" shouted Frank. "Yellow-bellied coward!"

"Go on, hit him," Suzie whispered again, and when Konrad still did not hit back she turned around and told Carol, "He must be chicken! Letting them say things and not doing anything!"

Carol was Suzie's best friend, and she always thought Suzie was right. "Yellow-bellied creampuff! Putting up with anything!" she said.

"He's just a baby!" said Suzie and Carol. "We're not playing with him!" And they sat down at the big table with Frank and Tony and played ludo.

"Would you like to help me play with my doll?" Kitty asked Konrad.

"Yes please," said Konrad. "Only you'll have to show me how. I only know how to play with trains and blocks and look at books."

Kitty fetched her new golden-haired doll and her doll's stroller and the tea set Konrad had brought her for a birthday present. She cleared a corner of the room, put the stroller in it, put the tea set on a little table and pretended to be pouring tea out of the pot into the cups. "You're the father and I'm the mother," she said, "and that's our baby in the stroller. Do you think you understand the game all right?"

Konrad got the idea at once. "I'm Mr. Thomas the druggist and you're Mrs. Bartolotti?"

Kitty nodded.

Soon Konrad was very good at playing fathers and mothers and babies, in fact, Kitty told him he played it better than anyone else she knew. However, Tony would keep interrupting them every few minutes. He was still sitting at the table with the others, and he was eating nuts and throwing the nutshells at Konrad and Kitty, shouting, "Dummy Bartolotti with the meatball eyes."

Konrad looked despairingly at Kitty. "Do *you* want me to hit him too?" he asked.

"Only if you want to very, very much," said Kitty. Konrad was relieved.

"I know," said Kitty. "Let's pretend it's very hot summer, and we're out in the country where there are a whole lot of flies, and every time a nutshell comes over it's another fly."

Konrad thought that was a good idea, so whenever a nutshell came sailing through the air he and Kitty cried,

"Oh dear, oh dear, another fly! What a terrible year for flies!" And they giggled. Tony got so annoyed he went home, shouting, "Meathead!" as he left. He meant Kitty as well as Konrad. He had decided he didn't want Kitty for a girl friend anymore.

At six o'clock Mrs. Robertson came into the living room, switched on the television and said the birthday party was over. Kitty went to see her guests off. As Suzie and Carol left they said, "Whatever can you see in that creampuff, Kitty?"

"What a dumb party!" said Frank. "And all because of that dummy!" He punched Konrad in the stomach again, since by now he was quite sure Konrad wouldn't punch him back. However, he hadn't reckoned on Kitty. Kitty shouted, "Stop it!" and with that she drove one fist into Frank's stomach, walloped him on the head with the other and kicked his shins.

Frank ran out of the building, howling and yelling, "I'm never coming to see you anymore! I'll get you, I swear I will!"

"Well!" said Suzie. "How about that! She's even doing his fighting for him now!"

"I suppose he's her new boy friend!" said Carol. And Suzie and Carol both left.

Kitty went up to the door of Mrs. Bartolotti's apartment on the third floor with Konrad.

"That girl said I must be your new boy friend," said Konrad, quietly.

"So you are, too," said Kitty, quietly.

"Am I? No kidding?"

"No kidding." Kitty nodded seriously.

Konrad hesitated. "Kitty, you're not just saying that so you won't hurt my feelings, are you?"

"Not a chance!" Kitty laughed. "I do like you, honest, I like you a whole lot. I like you better than anyone else!"

"I'm glad," said Konrad, quietly.

"Tomorrow we'll go to school together," said Kitty, "and we'll come home together, and after school we'll go to the park, and if anyone tries to belt you they'll have me to deal with! They'll watch it, you just see! I'm very strong."

"Thank you," said Konrad. He rang the bell, and Kitty ran down to the second floor again, waving to him once from the stairs.

"Was it fun?" asked Mrs. Bartolotti, opening the door for Konrad.

"Some of it wasn't," said Konrad, "but some of it was great!"

"That's how life generally is," said Mrs. Bartolotti, and she took Konrad into the kitchen. There was tuna salad and black bread and licorice sticks for supper. Mrs. Bartolotti had forgotten to go shopping again. As Konrad spread tuna on a slice of bread he asked, "Is it right for a girl to protect a boy? Shouldn't it be the other way around?"

Mrs. Bartolotti was sucking a licorice stick. "It doesn't make a bit of difference, Konrad," she said, still sucking. "It's all nonsense about boys having to do the protecting! The important thing is for the person who needs protection to get it."

"But don't you think some people might laugh?" Konrad persisted.

Mrs. Bartolotti took the licorice stick out of her mouth, dipped it in the tuna salad and licked it off. "Oh, Konrad!" she said. "Now, you listen to me! Some things in this world are far more important than other things, and one thing there is no need to bother about at all is what other people say!"

Mrs. Bartolotti dipped the licorice stick back in the tuna and mixed the salad absentmindedly with it. "If you keep wondering what other people would do," she went on, "and you always do the same as them, you'll end up being just like them, and then you won't be able to stand your own company." Mrs. Bartolotti stopped mixing the tuna salad, looked at Konrad and asked, "Do you understand?"

"Not really," said Konrad, taking a mouthful of bread and tuna. "But Kitty's going to be my girl friend."

"Well, fancy that!" cried Mrs. Bartolotti, delighted. "We must have a little drink to celebrate!"

"Oh, Mother!" Konrad shook his head.

"Sorry!" said Mrs. Bartolotti. "I mean, *I* must have a little drink to celebrate!" And she got out the whiskey bottle and poured herself a drink.

"Well, all the best to you, Konrad!" she said, draining the glass.

Just as Mrs. Bartolotti was putting her empty glass down on the kitchen table there was a ring at the door. Three short rings in quick succession, all very gentle. Mrs. Bartolotti sighed.

"I wonder who that is?" said Konrad.

Mrs. Bartolotti stood up slowly and went to the door.

"Three short rings, all very gentle," she said, "is always Thomas the druggist."

Mr. Thomas the druggist followed Bertie Bartolotti into the kitchen. He was carrying an enormous plastic shopping bag, which he put down by the kitchen door. He stared at the remains of supper on the kitchen table with disgust.

"Anything wrong?" asked Mrs. Bartolotti.

Mr. Thomas raised his right forefinger and waggled it in front of Mrs. Bartolotti's nose. "Protein, animal protein, that's what a boy of seven needs," he said. "Not licorice! Boys of seven also need Vitamins A, B, C and D."

"All right, he can have them tomorrow!" snapped Mrs. Bartolotti, removing his waggling forefinger from in front of her nose.

"He can have them today!" said Mr. Thomas, picking up the big plastic shopping bag. He took out a packet of Rye Crisp, an apple and a piece of cheese. "Now, Konrad, this is the right kind of supper for a growing boy!" he said.

"Thank you very much," said Konrad, not very happily, since he had already put himself outside four large slices of bread and tuna, and three licorice sticks.

"He's already had supper," said Mrs. Bartolotti.

"That was not *supper*, my dear, that was an insult to the digestive system," said Mr. Thomas, pushing the cheese and crackers across the table to Konrad. "Things will have to change here, my dear. All sorts of things," he said.

Mrs. Bartolotti looked grimly at him. "Such as what, may I ask?"

Mr. Thomas cleared several small objects—hairpins, a

spoon, a couple of leaves of chives and a pair of nail scissors—off the kitchen stool, and sat down. You could tell he was about to launch into a long speech. You could also tell he was a little bit scared of saying just what things would have to change.

"Such as what?" repeated Mrs. Bartolotti, looking at him more grimly than ever.

Mr. Thomas the druggist blinked rapidly, rubbed his hand, and began. "My dear, you are a very sweet, charming woman, but not at all a suitable person to raise a child of Konrad's quality. And so I have decided to raise him myself."

Mrs. Bartolotti laughed. Not a pleasant laugh—in fact, a very nasty laugh. Then she really let him have it. "Oh, so you've decided, have you? All very fine, I must say! You know what you can do, you and your decisions? You go and have a child yourself! Or order one. You can do what you like with the poor little thing as far as I'm concerned! Bring him up any way you fancy. I don't care! But just you leave my Konrad alone, you nothing, you! You apology for a person! You germ!"

You could hardly say Mr. Thomas didn't bat an eyelid, because he batted them both, but he stayed put on the kitchen stool. "My dear," he went on, "you can insult me as much as you like, but when my son's welfare is at stake, I shall stand firm!"

Mrs. Bartolotti jumped up, went to the drawer, got out the blue envelope containing Konrad's documents, plunged her shaking fingers into it and produced Konrad's birth certificate. "Look at this, will you!" she shouted. "What does it say there? Does it say Thomas the druggist? No! Konrad Augustus Bartolotti, that's what it says. Father: Konrad Augustus Bartolotti!"

But Mr. Thomas did not seem at all impressed. He said Konrad had voluntarily accepted him as a father, and he had agreed to Konrad's choice. Moreover, Mr. Bartolotti had been in Katmandu for some years now, and thus was not around to be a father in any real sense of the word. And what's more, Mrs. Bartolotti herself had recognized him as Konrad's father, since she had asked him for child support. "And whoever pays child support is the father," said Mr. Thomas.

Bertie Bartolotti felt like calling Mr. Thomas some more names; indeed, she felt like flinging him out of the apartment—simply grabbing him under the arms, dragging him across the kitchen and through the hall and throwing him out the door. However, she did not, because at that point Mr. Thomas put his hand in the big plastic shopping bag again and produced a ball-point pen, notebooks, crayons, felt-tip pens and a red schoolbag.

"Oh, thank you!" cried Konrad. He picked the things up and admired them. He took the top off the ball-point pen and wrote KONRAD BARTOLOTTI on the blanks for his name on the notebooks.

"Or has your mother already bought you pens and pencils and so on for school?" asked Mr. Thomas, spitefully. "Not the kind of thing a good mother would forget, is it?"

"No, I haven't bought anything yet," said Bertie Bartolotti, getting red in the face because she was ashamed of herself. Being ashamed of herself made her even angrier. "Who cares about pens and things!" she said. "As if there wasn't anything more important in the world than note-books and stupid crayons and a red schoolbag!"

"Oh, Mom!" said Konrad, horrified. "You mustn't say things like that!" He had tears in his eyes.

"I want Konrad to move in with me," said Mr. Thomas. "I have a greater sense of responsibility than you, and more money. I can hire a first-class housekeeper to take care of him, and send him to a first-class private school, and he can have a first-class . . ."

"You," Mrs. Bartolotti interrupted him, "are a first-class fool!"

Konrad was crying properly now. Big tears were rolling down his cheeks and dripping onto the crackers and cheese. Mr. Thomas took a clean handkerchief out of his coat pocket, wiped Konrad's nose, mopped up his cheeks and told Mrs. Bartolotti, "There, *now* see how fit you are to bring up a child!" And then he asked Konrad, "Well, how about moving in with me, my son?"

Konrad sat perfectly still, looking at the kitchen table.

Mr. Thomas waited. He blinked nervously, and the frown lines on his forehead twitched.

"I don't know what to do," Konrad said at last. "Back at the factory nobody thought of this kind of family situation happening."

"Konrad!" Mrs. Bartolotti took a deep breath and tried to keep her voice slow and calm. She succeeded. "Konrad, if you don't know what to do, you must listen to your own heart and then you'll *feel* what you really want."

Of course, Konrad did feel something—he felt a number of things, in fact. He felt that he liked Mrs. Bartolotti very much, and he liked Mr. Thomas very much too. He felt he was sad when they quarreled. He felt that he couldn't possibly decide between Mrs. Bartolotti and Mr. Thomas.

Mrs. Bartolotti picked up her pocketbook and scuffled around in it for her cigar case. She took out the longest, fattest cigar it contained; she was badly in need of a cigar. She lit it, thinking, How can I get Konrad to say he'll stay with me? Mrs. Bartolotti inhaled deeply three times, and Mr. Thomas waved the smoke away from Konrad's nose with his handkerchief, which was wet with tears. "Contaminating the atmosphere," he muttered. "When Konrad comes to live with me he will breathe clean, nicotine-free air." Mrs. Bartolotti inhaled deeply three times twice more, and then she knew how to persuade Konrad to stay.

"Thomas, what do you think of Kitty Robertson?" asked Mrs. Bartolotti innocently.

"A very rude, naughty, badly behaved child!" said Mr. Thomas. "The other day she kept jumping on and off the scales in the shop, and she has a bad habit of sticking her tongue out at me! We must take care she doesn't have anything to do with Konrad."

"But suppose she wants to be his girl friend?" asked Mrs. Bartolotti, even more innocently.

"I would soon put a stop to anything like that!" said Mr. Thomas firmly.

As Mr. Thomas spoke, Konrad had gone very pale. Alarmingly pale.

"Don't you feel well, my boy?" asked Mr. Thomas, worried. He was afraid the mixture of licorice and tuna fish had upset Konrad's stomach.

"I'm quite all right, thank you," said Konrad. "But I know what I do feel. I feel I'd like to stay with my mother."

Mrs. Bartolotti heaved a sigh of relief.

Mr. Thomas looked sad. "Don't you like me anymore?" he asked.

"Oh yes, Dad, of course I like you!" said Konrad, "I like you very much, really I do. I'll always be glad when you come to see me, honest!"

Mr. Thomas believed Konrad, but he was not pleased. Indeed, he was quite angry, and soon he went home.

Chapter Seven ────────

Konrad had been living with Mrs. Bartolotti for over three weeks now. Every weekday Kitty would wait for him on the second floor at quarter to nine in the morning, and they went to school together. Almost every morning they would find Tony standing on the corner waiting for them, and he would run along behind them muttering, "Watch out, I'll get you!" Frank would be waiting on the corner where they turned into Main Street, ready to fall in beside Tony and call Konrad names. He would chant: "Sucker, stinker, numbskull, know-it-all, creampuff, canary, fathead, greaseball, blubber-brain stooge!" and end with, "Stoolie, yellow ape, go home to the zoo!"

However, Frank and Tony kept their distance, and they did not throw any nutshells or plum pits either. They were too scared of Kitty.

On the days she came out of school at the same time as Konrad, Kitty protected him on the way home too. But since she was in third grade, a class below him, she finished school half an hour earlier on Mondays, Wednesdays and Fridays. Kitty would have been quite happy to wait for Konrad by the lockers or outside school, and in fact she had

done so, twice, but Mrs. Robertson had been angry, and there had been trouble.

"You're to be home fifteen minutes after school is out, at the latest!" cried Mrs. Robertson. "Not a moment later, or you'll be sorry!"

Mrs. Robertson added that she thought it was ridiculous for a girl to be protecting a boy.

"Not that I have anything against little Konrad," she said. "He's a very well-mannered, polite, intelligent child, and he knows all the answers in your quiz game, and says good morning very politely. Still, I should have thought he could look after himself!"

"What's more," she added, as an afterthought, "it seems very strange for that peculiar woman to have such a well-mannered child, and I would like to know where she got him from out of the blue."

Kitty knew where Konrad had come from because he had told her. She had promised not to breathe a word to anyone, so she did not tell her mother.

All this meant that Konrad had to go home on his own on Monday, Wednesday and Friday, though "alone" was not really the right word, since he had half 4A running after him. Frank was not scared to touch him if Kitty was not around. He threw pebbles at Konrad, tried to trip him up, punched him in the stomach or kicked his bottom. The other children did not interfere; they hated Konrad. Their teacher, Mrs. Stone, used to tell them at least three times every lesson, "Why don't you try to be like Konrad?" The others did not like that. If everyone else in the c̸ had something wrong, Mrs. Stone would say, "I e̸ Konrad's got it right." And sure enough, Konrad̸

have it right, and the other children did not like that either. What was more, Konrad knew how to spell everything, he had beautiful handwriting, he gave the right emphasis to every part of a sentence when he was reading out loud, he sat still at his desk, he didn't chatter, he never ate during lessons, he never chewed gum and of course he never pulled long strings of gum out of his mouth. He was always looking at Mrs. Stone and listening to what she was saying. Not surprisingly, all that drove the other children wild. If only he'd been bad at games and sports, like some model pupils! But no! He was also the only kid in the class who could climb the rope right up to the ceiling of the gym in a flash, and he had a singing voice described by Mrs. Stone as "clear as a bell and pure as an angel—it does your heart good to hear him!"

Konrad could also draw a car so well that you could tell right away if it was a Ford T-Bird or a Ford Granada.

"A perfect pupil . . . that was about all we needed!" said the other children in the class, adding, "Slimy little grind. We don't want *him* here!"

And Konrad was so ignorant and inexperienced that he made a great many mistakes when he tried playing with ordinary children, talking to them or just getting along with them. On his second day at school there was an arithmetic test in the third period, and Freddy, who was sitting next to Konrad, whispered, "What's twelve times twelve minus seventeen plus thirty-six?" Konrad hadn't answered because Mrs. Stone had said, "I don't want to hear anyone speak a single word during the test!" When Freddy, who was very bad at arithmetic, asked under his breath three more times, Konrad finally said, "But I don't think

I'm supposed to tell you the answer." That had made Freddy hopping mad, and after that he disliked Konrad as much as Frank did.

Next day Annette hit the window at the back of the classroom with her ruler, and a windowpane cracked. The teacher had just gone out of the room for a moment, and when she came back and saw the crack in the pane she insisted on being told who had done it. No one spoke up, and Annette dug around in her schoolbag acting as if she were perfectly innocent. Mrs. Stone asked several children, "Do you know who did it?" and they all pretended not to know. At last she asked Konrad. "Konrad, did you see who did it? If you did see, Konrad, then it's your duty to tell me." So Konrad said it was Annette. A buzz of disgust went right through the class, but Mrs. Stone was very pleased.

On Konrad's fifth day in school Mrs. Stone made him sit at her desk to keep an eye on the class whenever she had to leave the room between periods, or go into another teacher's room. He had to see that no one went up to the open window, no one left the classroom, no one talked out loud and no one started a fight.

At first the other kids did not take Konrad seriously. They went up to the open window, they fought, they went out of the room and they talked out loud. But when they realized Konrad was writing down all the naughty things they did so that Mrs. Stone could punish them later on, they were very angry indeed, and they despised Konrad.

Mr. Thomas the druggist spoke to Mrs. Stone at a PTA

meeting, and was proud to hear that Konrad was "a real sweetheart" and "the kind of pupil every teacher dreams of having." As for Mrs. Bertie Bartolotti, she had no idea at all what Konrad did in school, or what the other children thought of him. She was not interested in what went on in school, though every day, when he came home, she asked, "Well, how were things today?"

Konrad always said, "All right, thank you, and the teacher was pleased with me." That was good enough for Mrs. Bartolotti; she felt glad he had a nice time at school, and thought no more about it.

Of course, Kitty Robertson knew about the way Konrad acted at school; he told her. So did the other kids. "Know what Bartolotti did today?" they would ask.

And after school, when Konrad went to Kitty's apartment or Kitty went to Konrad's, she would ask, "Konrad, why didn't you tell Freddy the answer to twelve times twelve minus seventeen plus thirty-six?" And, "Konrad, you shouldn't write it down when the kids go out of the room!" But Konrad just shook his head. "I honestly don't like doing it, Kitty," he said. "But they're doing things they aren't allowed to do, so it's my duty to report them. The teacher said so, and I have to do my duty!"

Kitty tried to make Konrad see that the other children would never be friends with him if he went on like this. She talked and talked and talked to him, but Konrad just shook his head unhappily. "It's no good, Kitty," he said. "That's the way I'm made. They trained me to be like that in the Final Preparation Department too. I just can't be any different!"

"Try, just for once. To please me!" said Kitty. Because Kitty herself found it was hard to have a friend whom everyone else hated.

So to please Kitty, Konrad tried. He tried in PT when the children wanted to swing on the rings, but the teacher wanted them to walk along the bar. "Come along, now!" called Mrs. Stone, but the children whispered to each other, "We'll go on strike! No balancing on the bars." They sat down on the floor, crossed their legs and did not move. Konrad sat on the floor and crossed his legs too.

"Hurry up, please!" said Mrs. Stone. The children did not budge. Konrad did not budge either. Kitty wants me not to, he thought. And the children want me not to! But then the teacher looked Konrad right in the eye and said, "Konrad, what do you think you're doing? I'd never have expected *you* to behave like this, Konrad!"

Konrad longed to stay put, but it was no good. He felt as if someone were grabbing him and yanking him to his feet, and he was unable to resist.

"Huh!" said the others. Konrad was standing up now.

"Strike-breaker! Scab!" hissed the other children. But Konrad was walking along the bar.

"Very good, Konrad," said the teacher.

"Konrad's a dirty rat," muttered the other children.

As a punishment, the others had to run around in a circle for ten minutes. Konrad spent those ten minutes sitting on a bench. The children cast angry glances at him as they panted past, and Konrad had tears in his eyes.

"Aren't you ashamed to be friends with a mean sneak like that?" the children asked Kitty after school that day.

Kitty defended Konrad. "He's not really a sneak. Honestly he isn't!" she would say. But since she couldn't tell the children where Konrad came from, and why he was like that, they did not believe her. Kitty could understand how they felt. She thought, If I'd only known Konrad at school I wouldn't be able to stand him either.

And every day Kitty told Konrad, "Konrad, you're going to have to change!"

Chapter Eight ————————

One afternoon Kitty and Konrad were sitting with Mrs. Bartolotti in her living room. Kitty had brought the quiz game up with her, and since both children knew all the answers by heart now, they were asking Mrs. Bartolotti the questions on the cards. Mrs. Bartolotti was sitting in her rocking chair, rocking gently back and forth, eating pickled herrings out of a big glass jar, painting her toenails bright blue from time to time, and getting all the answers wrong.

Kitty laughed till she cried when Mrs. Bartolotti said, "Where's the Leaning Tower? Oh, in Kalamazoo, I should think—all the gates and buildings and things there lean over sideways." As for the square root of numbers, Bertie Bartolotti had no idea whatsoever about them. "Roots?" she said. "Trees have roots. Flowers have roots. Parsnips are roots, and you can make parsnip wine out of them." She painted another toenail, sighed because she had got nail polish over half her toe too, and said, "But parsnips are pointed. I never heard of roots being square. Did you say a hundred and forty-four has a root? I wonder what sort of wine it would make?"

"The square root of four is two," Konrad explained.

"And the square root of nine is three, and the square root of sixteen is four."

"Just think of them—two and three and four—all buried in the ground!" said Mrs. Bartolotti cheerfully. Konrad was about to go on explaining square roots when the doorbell rang. In fact, it rang three times. It was the mailman with a registered special-delivery letter. The envelope was large and stiff and sky blue. It looked just like the envelope that had held the letter inside Konrad's tin can, and there was no return address on it.

Mrs. Bartolotti looked at the letter, and looked at Konrad, and looked back at the letter.

"Who's it from?" asked Kitty curiously.

Mrs. Bartolotti put the letter in her bathrobe pocket. "Oh, it's only junk mail," she said.

"Junk mail doesn't come by registered special delivery!" Kitty pointed out.

"Mom, that letter's from the factory, isn't it?" said Konrad. "It's all right to talk about it in front of Kitty; she knows about me."

"Oh please, *please,* open the letter!" said Kitty.

Mrs. Bartolotti hesitated. "But supposing it's something nasty?" she said. Mrs. Bartolotti preferred to give unpleasantness as wide a berth as possible. She never opened letters from the income tax office at all. "Let's forget about the letter," she suggested. "If we burn it, it will be as if it never came!"

"But perhaps the letter says something nice," suggested Kitty. "Perhaps Konrad's been left a big inheritance or something."

Mrs. Bartolotti put her hand in her bathrobe pocket and felt the letter. "Oh, children," she murmured. "There isn't anything nice in this letter, I can feel it in my fingertips. It feels very nasty indeed to me."

"Then we *must* open it—now!" said Kitty. She added that nasty things you know about aren't half as bad as nasty things you don't know about.

Mrs. Bartolotti took the sky-blue letter out of her pocket and handed it to Kitty.

"You read it, Kitty," she said. "I don't dare!"

Kitty opened the sky-blue envelope, took out a folded sheet of sky-blue paper, unfolded it and read out loud:

Dear Mrs. Bartolotti:

We have discovered, in the process of checking the records of our Delivery Department, that an unfortunate error has occurred. Through a fault in the operation of our computer, some goods were mistakenly dispatched to you, namely, a seven-year-old boy. As you have no claim to these goods we would ask you to return same to us directly.

The order form completed by you was for two memory aids, "Memoria" brand. We ceased production of these some time ago and therefore regret that we are unable to supply them.

We would ask you to have the boy in readiness for us at once. Our Service Department will collect him at the earliest possible date for delivery to the correct parents.

We would also point out to you that in all eventualities Instant Children remain the property of the manu-

*facturers throughout their lives, and are merely leased
to parents for use and rearing, on the same principle as
the renting of a telephone.*

*Any objections on your part would therefore be fu-
tile, nor would there be any point in your taking the
matter to court.*

Again, we offer our apologies for the error.

Yours sincerely . . .

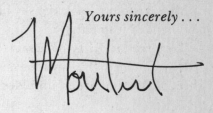

Kitty stumbled over the next word and stopped. She
peered at the paper. "The signature looks like Honbert
or Monbert," she said. "I can't make it out."

"Never mind the signature!" cried Bertie Bartolotti, in
a trembling voice. She looked quite green in spite of all
the blue and red and pink makeup on her face, and she
seemed much smaller and thinner than usual. "They'll be
coming in a day or so," she said quietly. "Just a day or
so . . ."

"You're not going to give Konrad back, are you?" cried
Kitty.

Mrs. Bartolotti took a handkerchief out of her bathrobe
pocket, blew her nose, snuffled into the hanky and said,
"But he belongs to someone else, and I don't have any
right to him, and it was two memory aids I really ordered!"

She blew her nose again and snuffled some more. "And
anyway I don't cook proper meals," she went on. "And I

wear crazy clothes, and I'm not a good mother, like Thomas says."

All this time Konrad had been sitting perfectly still, not saying a word. Now he jumped up, and shouted in the loudest voice the others had ever heard from him, "You *are* a good mother, and you're *my* mother!"

"There you are!" said Kitty. "It's you he wants!"

Mrs. Bartolotti blew her nose and went on snuffling into her hanky. She was sobbing as she said, "But you could go to a mother who'd give you vitamins, and knows the right sort of songs to sing, and understands square roots and has a real husband to be a father to you."

Konrad shook his head. "I've grown to love you and Mr. Thomas," he said. "And if I went somewhere else I'd never see Kitty again." He was shaking his head quite hard now. "No, I want to stay here. I can *feel* I want to stay here."

"Is that what you really feel?" cried Bertie Bartolotti. She jumped up from her rocking chair, and she did not look so small and thin and green in the face anymore. She picked Konrad up and kissed him on both cheeks and on his neck, his forehead and his ears, in fact anywhere there was enough skin showing to be kissed. Then she put him down again and cried, "Well then, we must think of an idea. A way to stop them getting him back. We must *do* something!"

"Write them a polite letter saying I want to stay here," Konrad suggested.

"That's no good," said Kitty. "People who'd write a letter like this . . ." She picked up the sky-blue sheet of paper from the table and tore it into tiny pieces. ". . . People who'd write a letter like this aren't going to care what you want, Konrad!"

"She's right!" said Bertie Bartolotti. "We must think of something brilliant."

Konrad looked very sad. "But if it's something forbidden I can't do it!" he said. "You know how it is, Kitty—I simply can't!"

"Forbidden!" cried Mrs. Bartolotti. "Who cares what that stupid factory says?"

"You two don't," said Konrad, quietly. "But I can't help it. That's the way they trained me to be!"

Mrs. Bartolotti lit a big cigar and inhaled deeply three times. She also blew two smoke rings in the air three times.

"She's thinking," said Konrad.

"It's all right, Konrad. I've thought!" Mrs. Bartolotti jumped up from her rocking chair and pointed to the bedroom door. "Go along, Konrad, go in there for a minute. There's something I have to discuss with Kitty."

"But why . . . ?"

Mrs. Bartolotti interrupted him. "Don't ask why, just obey your mother! You've learned to be good and obedient, haven't you? Well, we've got to discuss something that children who aren't allowed to do anything forbidden mustn't hear."

So Konrad went into the bedroom and shut the door behind him.

Mrs. Bartolotti, however, leaned down close to Kitty's ear and started whispering to her. Kitty's face began to beam. "That's a great idea!" she cried, when Mrs. Bartolotti had finished. "Yes, of course I'll help you!"

Scarcely an hour after the mailman had delivered the

registered special-delivery letter, Kitty went down to her mother in the second-floor apartment. "Please, Mom, can I help Mrs. Bartolotti take her big rug to the cleaners?" she asked.

Mrs. Robertson hesitated. She really wanted to go to the photographer's to get a picture of Kitty taken for Aunt Emma's birthday.

"But we can go to the photographer's tomorrow. Please!" Kitty begged. "It's such a heavy rug, and poor Mrs. Bartolotti will never be able to carry it all by herself."

"Why doesn't Konrad help her?" asked Mrs. Robertson. Then she got a big surprise, because Kitty said, "Konrad? Oh, he isn't living with Mrs. Bartolotti anymore, Mom."

"Good gracious me! Whatever happened?"

"Well, I don't exactly know, but if I help Mrs. Bartolotti carry her rug I expect she'll tell me."

Mrs. Robertson was as curious as the next person, and it was quite true, she *could* take Kitty to the photographer's tomorrow. And it really would be a shame not to give poor Mrs. Bartolotti a hand with her rug.

"Very well, dear," said Mrs. Robertson. "But don't ask about Konrad too obviously—that's not polite."

Kitty had reached the door when Mrs. Robertson added, "He was still here this morning, though. He went to school with you."

"No, you're wrong, Mom," Kitty said. "I walked to school with Tony." And she ran out of the apartment before Mrs. Robertson could ask any more questions.

She went upstairs again. Mrs. Bartolotti was waiting on the other side of her front door. "Let's get a move on," she said. "In case they take it into their nasty heads to come today."

They went into the living room and pulled the big rug out from under the rocking chair. Then they dragged it into the bedroom. Konrad was perched on the edge of the bed. "May I listen again now?" he asked.

"You may lie down on the rug, Konrad," said Mrs. Bartolotti. So Konrad lay down on the rug, and Mrs. Bartolotti wrapped it around him. It went around Konrad three times. Then Kitty and Mrs. Bartolotti picked the rug up. Mrs. Bartolotti took one end under her arm, and Kitty put the other end over her shoulder.

"Got enough air in there?" Kitty called down into the roll of rug.

"Yes, I'm all right," said a hollow voice from inside.

"Off we go, then," said Kitty. "Take small steps, please, or we'll get out of step, and it will sway about, and Konrad will feel seasick."

"Right," said Mrs. Bartolotti.

They marched out of the house, keeping in step, down the street and off to the dry cleaners.

Mrs. Robertson was standing at her living-room window watching. "It's quite true," she said to herself. "Konrad isn't with them!" And she went next door to see her neighbor, Mrs. March. "What do you think?" she told Mrs. March. "Mrs. Bartolotti's Konrad has left! Several days ago!"

"But this very morning I saw . . ."

"Oh no, that was Tony," said Mrs. Robertson.

The dry cleaners was next to Mr. Thomas's drugstore. Kitty and Mrs. Bartolotti went in with their roll of rug.

"Good afternoon," said the woman behind the counter.

"How much would it cost to clean this rug?" asked Mrs. Bartolotti.

The woman felt one corner of the rug, to test the wool and the weave. "Fifty cents per square foot," she said.

"Too much," said Kitty, winking at Mrs. Bartolotti.

"So sorry to have troubled you!" said Mrs. Bartolotti to the woman. "Come along, honey, let's go home again," she told Kitty.

They walked straight through the shop with the roll of rug, but not to the front door—they were making for the door at the back of the shop, which led into the hall of the whole big building.

"Er . . . where are you going?" asked the woman.

"We live on the third floor of this building," said Kitty. "It's quicker this way."

The woman had been working in this particular branch of the cleaners for only three weeks, so she did not know all the people who lived in the upstairs apartments of the building yet. She opened the back door and let Kitty and Mrs. Bartolotti out into the hall. A customer happened to come in just then, so the woman closed the door at once, and saw no more of Mrs. Bartolotti and Kitty, who were not going up to the third floor at all. Instead, they were ringing the bell at the back door of the drugstore.

Mrs. Bartolotti rang the bell very loud and long. After all, Mr. Thomas would be in the front of the store selling odds and ends. He did hear the back doorbell ring, but he thought, Whoever it is, they can just come around to the front!

Finally, however, the long, loud ringing irritated Mr. Thomas, and he said to the woman he was waiting on,

"One moment, if you don't mind! There's someone at the back door." He went through the first room behind the store and the second room behind the store, into the third room behind the store, where the back door was. He was going to say indignantly, "You've got some nerve, ringing my bell like that!" to whoever it was, but he never had a chance. As he opened the door, Mrs. Bartolotti pushed him aside, dragging the rug into the third room behind the store, while Kitty made her way in after her and closed the door. Then Mrs. Bartolotti pushed the empty cardboard cartons and crates of baby formula away, until she had enough space to unroll the rug.

"What on earth is all this?" asked Mr. Thomas, horrified.

"Got to be hidden," said Mrs. Bartolotti, beginning to unroll the rug.

"Why on earth should I hide your living-room rug?"

"Not the rug! You've got to hide Konrad!"

"Where is Konrad?"

Mrs. Bartolotti sighed; he was being so slow! "In the rug, of course, you fool!"

She had unrolled the rug completely by now, and there was Konrad, lying in the middle of it, rather tired and extremely dusty, because the rug really did need cleaning.

"Sit down and I'll tell you all about it," Mrs. Bartolotti told Mr. Thomas.

"But the store is full of people, my dear!" said Mr. Thomas.

"Tell them to go away and shut the store, then!" Mrs. Bartolotti demanded.

"But that would attract far too much attention, Mrs. Bartolotti!" Kitty said. "You don't just shut a drugstore like that! People would all wonder why."

I must say, young Kitty isn't quite as stupid as I thought! Mr. Thomas thought to himself.

They could hear a babble of impatient voices coming from the front of the store through the two open doors of the other rooms.

"Where are you, Mr. Thomas?" called a woman's voice. "I'm in a hurry!"

Mr. Thomas went back into the store.

"Oh, well, if he can't talk to me in here I'll go out there and talk to him!" said Mrs. Bartolotti. She picked up a white coat hanging on a hook and put it on.

Konrad was still sitting in the middle of the rug, coughing because he had breathed in so much dust as they carried him, and trying to clean the dirt off his face and hands with a handkerchief.

"Look here, my dear, this really won't do . . ." Mr. Thomas whispered to the white-robed figure of Mrs. Bartolotti, who was standing at the counter beside him.

"Oh yes, it will," Mrs. Bartolotti whispered back, picking up a mortar and pestle and working away energetically, as if she had to crush some very hard pills to a very fine powder. And as Mr. Thomas took prescriptions and money, and handed over the customers' packages and change, she whispered her news to him. "We only got Konrad by mistake. They're coming to take him away."

"Good heavens—how awful!" Mr. Thomas was so upset that he said that out loud, and the man who had just handed over his prescription thought it was meant for him. "Why?" he asked anxiously. "It's for my blood pressure. Is it harmful?"

"I'm so sorry," Mr. Thomas apologized to the man. He whispered to Mrs. Bartolotti, "Did you actually pay for Konrad?"

"No," said Mrs. Bartolotti, and she whispered the whole story to Mr. Thomas, everything the sky-blue letter had said.

The customers, who all knew Mr. Thomas as a quiet but friendly sort of man, were rather surprised, because he simply handed them their packages and change and never said good afternoon, or even asked how they were. When one woman wanted to be weighed on the big scales he just said she couldn't, and when a man asked whether Mr. Thomas was sure the medicine the doctor had prescribed for him wasn't unpleasant, he paid no attention at all.

When Mrs. Bartolotti, still working away with the mortar and pestle, had finished whispering her story, she asked, "Well, will you help me?"

"Of course! You can count on me," said Mr. Thomas. "That's only natural!" He happened to be handing a mother a bottle of cough syrup just then, and she was very pleased, because she believed that natural plant extracts were best for a cough.

Mrs. Bartolotti put the mortar back on its shelf, whispering, "I'll take him upstairs," and went back through the two other rooms to rejoin Konrad and Kitty.

"It's all right!" she called.

There was an iron spiral staircase beside one wall of the third room at the back, leading up to Mr. Thomas's living room on the second floor. Mrs. Bartolotti, Konrad and Kitty climbed the spiral staircase.

"How horrible!" muttered Kitty, when she saw Mr. Thomas's living room. It was stuffed full of old furniture. The windows had heavy, shabby, red velvet curtains, and there was a black silk tablecloth with long tassels on the table.

"What are we doing here, Mom?" asked Konrad.

"Well, Kitty and I are going home now," said Mrs. Bartolotti, "and you must wait here for Mr. Thomas. He'll come up as soon as he's closed for the day."

"Will you be able to stand it here, in this musty old room?" asked Kitty.

"A boy of seven should be able to amuse himself for a couple of hours," said Konrad bravely, and he went over to the bookshelf and took out Volume *Katmandu–Longinus* of the encyclopedia. "There are several things beginning with *K* I don't know about yet," he said, sitting down in an ancient old armchair and opening the volume.

As for Mrs. Bartolotti and Kitty, they went back down the spiral staircase, quickly rolled up the rug again, and dragged it through the back door into the hall. Kitty rang the dry cleaners' back doorbell.

The woman opened the door. "What is it this time?" she asked.

"I've changed my mind," said Mrs. Bartolotti. "I will have it cleaned after all." And she thrust the roll of rug into the woman's arms and went out with Kitty through the front of the shop again.

The woman stapled a number to the rug and leaned it

up in the corner. "Some people are very odd!" she said to herself.

When Mrs. Bartolotti and Kitty came out of the cleaners' front door Mrs. Robertson happened to be looking out of the window again. She saw them both. They were in there a long time! she thought. And then she thought, I do hope Kitty's found out why Konrad isn't with Mrs. Bartolotti anymore.

Kitty went home, and told her mother Konrad had disappeared without a trace four days earlier, and had probably gone to look for his real, natural father, Mr. Konrad Augustus Bartolotti, who had gone to Katmandu. At any rate, Konrad was nowhere to be found.

Mrs. Bartolotti went home too, and sat down at her frame, but she was thinking about Konrad so much she could not work. She sat there until nearly seven o'clock, smoking and thinking, and every half hour or so she would weave one tiny black thread into her rug.

About seven o'clock in the evening Mrs. Bartolotti jumped up, ran into the bathroom and washed all the makeup off her face. She put a gray scarf over her yellow hair, and dug about in the big closet in the hall for the gray knitted jacket Mr. Thomas had given her for Christmas. She had never worn the gray knitted jacket before, because gray was a color she hated. But now she put it on and looked in the mirror, telling her reflection, "My dear, you look all gray and ugly like a nasty old beetle. But at least no one will recognize you in this outfit!"

Sure enough, no one did recognize Mrs. Bartolotti. She went out of the building, and the superintendent was standing at the gate talking to the woman from the market. They didn't even look at Mrs. Bartolotti.

Mrs. Bartolotti went down the road to the drugstore, passing several people she knew, but none of them so much as glanced at her.

Even Mr. Thomas did not recognize Mrs. Bartolotti at first when she rang the doorbell of his apartment. He stared at her for a few seconds, and even asked, "What can I do for you, ma'am?" But when he did recognize her he was very pleased. "How nice you look today, my dear!" he said.

"Typical!" said Mrs. Bartolotti, crossly "I look like a nasty old beetle, and you say you like it!"

"I do like beetles better than parrots," murmured Mr. Thomas, taking Mrs. Bartolotti into the living room.

Konrad was there, sitting at the table with the black silk cloth. He had several volumes of the encyclopedia open in front of him. "I've learned about sixty-seven new things, Mom," he said, "and Dad has just tested me on them."

Mrs. Bartolotti slammed all the encyclopedia volumes shut and pushed them off the table. They fell to the floor with so many thuds. Then she swept the black silk cloth off the table too, because the sight of black made her feel quite ill, sat down, put her elbows on the table and said, "Right! Now I will reveal my great plan!"

Mr. Thomas sat down in an armchair, eager to hear the great plan, but Konrad was looking very depressed. "I'm sorry, Mom," he said, "but I don't think any plan will work. The people from the factory are very clever. They'd find me anywhere. They know thousands of tricks."

"They will not find you!" said Mrs. Bartolotti. "At least, it will be some time before they catch up with you, and by the time they find you, you won't be you anymore."

"What on earth do you mean?" said Mr. Thomas, jumping up.

"Sit down, Thomas, and listen to me!" Bertie Bartolotti told him. So he did sit down in his armchair again, and Bertie Bartolotti went on.

"Desperate situations call for desperate remedies, right?" Mr. Thomas and Konrad nodded in agreement. "Well!" Mrs. Bartolotti raised her right forefinger and waved it about in the air triumphantly. "Well . . . the Service Department people from the factory will be looking for a good, polite, nicely behaved, obedient Instant Boy. Exactly like the product they delivered." Mr. Thomas and Konrad nodded again. "So," said Mrs. Bartolotti, waving her right forefinger more violently than ever, "so we must change the product so radically that those people don't recognize it as one of theirs!"

"Are you going to dye his hair?" asked Mr. Thomas.

"Oh, don't be so silly!" Bertie Bartolotti looked at Mr. Thomas and shook her head. Then she turned to Konrad.

"What's the opposite of good?"

"Bad," said Konrad.

"And the opposite of obedient?"

"Disobedient."

"The opposite of quiet?"

"Noisy."

"The opposite of nicely behaved?"

"Naughty."

"And docile?"

"Rebellious."

"You see?" said Mrs. Bartolotti to Mr. Thomas. "Get him to be like *that,* and they won't recognize him anymore."

"Oh no!" cried Mr. Thomas, horrified.

"Well, do you want them to take him away?"

"Oh no!" cried Mr. Thomas, even more horrified.

"Then you must agree to a radical change in the product."

"Is it really necessary?" asked Mr. Thomas, sadly.

"Absolutely," said Mrs. Bartolotti firmly.

Konrad cleared his throat. "Please," he said quietly. "It's a very, very good plan, Mom, but you know I can't be any different from the way I am. I've tried already. I tried once to please Kitty, and it didn't work."

"Stuff and nonsense!" snorted Mrs. Bartolotti, and she told Konrad she had already had a long talk with Kitty about all that. "It's ridiculous to say you can't be any different," she added. "You weren't like that when they produced you—that was the way they taught you to be. In the Final Preparation Department. Well, now Kitty is going to re-educate you. They got you used to behaving one way, and Kitty is going to get you used to behaving differently."

"Do you really think it will work?" asked Konrad.

"We can try!" said Mrs. Bartolotti, and then she said good-bye to Mr. Thomas and Konrad, kissing Konrad three times on each cheek, because she knew she might not be seeing him again for some time.

Mrs. Bartolotti had a very restless night, with some horrible nightmares. She dreamed of two enormous gray men who came for Konrad, and Konrad tried to run away, but the men grabbed hold of him, and there was soft chewing gum all over the floor. Konrad couldn't run away because he was stuck in the chewing gum. Mrs. Bartolotti wanted to help him, but she stuck fast in the chewing gum too, and could not move from the spot.

When Mrs. Bartolotti had dreamed this horrible dream ten times running she decided to get up. She put her bathrobe on and went into the bathroom. It was still dark outside. Mrs. Bartolotti put her makeup on—a great deal of makeup—hoping all the lovely colors would make her feel better. Then she made a big pot of coffee, and sat down at the kitchen table to wait. She looked out the kitchen window and saw the sky slowly getting brighter and brighter. At first everything was quiet in the street down below, but when the sky was quite light, pink with apple-green streaks, cars began driving along the street, horns honking and tires squealing as they went around the curve.

Every time Bertie Bartolotti heard footsteps in the hall outside the door of her apartment she jumped. And every time the steps passed her door without stopping she breathed a sigh of relief.

As she was drinking her fourth cup of coffee there were more steps, but this time they did not pass her door. They stopped outside, and the doorbell rang. Mrs. Bartolotti felt like crawling away to hide. Under the table, or in the corner by the refrigerator.

But she told herself to be brave. If I don't answer now he'll only come back later, she thought.

The man outside her door was very small and thin. He

wore sky-blue overalls. Beside the man, standing on the doormat, was a very big, silvery can with a screw top.

He was going to take my Konrad away in that! thought Mrs. Bartolotti. The idea made her so furious that she stopped feeling frightened. "Yes, what is it?" she asked. As she was a good deal taller than the sky-blue man she was able to look down at him as she spoke.

"I've come to pick up the wrong delivery you had," said the little sky-blue man.

"Sorry," said Mrs. Bartolotti. "The wrong delivery I had ran away four days ago. Disappeared without a trace. Probably gone to Katmandu."

"Where?"

"Katmandu! Where his father went. His father as named on his birth certificate."

The little sky-blue man stood very upright, but that did not make him much taller. "You never should have allowed it!" he cried. "He is the property of my company!"

"Allowed it!" snorted Bertie Bartolotti. "Really! First you send me something I don't need and I don't want, and then you come and kick up a fuss about it!"

"Did you report the loss to the police?" asked the little sky-blue man.

"Now, you just listen to me, you little blue pygmy!" Bertie Bartolotti went right up to the little man. "Who do you think is going to bother with telling the police they've lost something they never wanted in the first place? You can just get back to your factory, you pygmy you!"

The sky-blue man took a step backward, grabbed his silvery can and ran for the stairs.

"I warn you, you'll be hearing from us again!" he said, running downstairs.

Mrs. Bartolotti closed the door of the apartment, then went to her living-room window and looked down at the street. She saw the little sky-blue man come out of the building, get into a sky-blue delivery truck with his can and drive off.

"But they'll be back, my dear," said Mrs. Bartolotti to herself. "Oh, you bet your sweet life they'll be back!"

Chapter Nine

As soon as school was over Kitty Robertson told her mother she was in a great hurry; she had to go and see her friend Joanne Miller. Kitty said Joanne was very bad at arithmetic, and she was going to teach her the multiplication table.

"Well, I'm glad to hear you're helping her," said Mrs. Robertson. She believed Kitty, because Joanne Miller really was extremely bad at arithmetic, and Kitty very seldom lied.

"But don't be home too late," said Mrs. Robertson.

"It'll be six or half-past before Joanne gets the hang of her three-times and four-times tables," said Kitty.

Konrad had spent the night in Mr. Thomas's bed while Mr. Thomas slept on the sofa in the living room. Konrad spent the morning learning new things out of the encyclopedia, Volume *Humidity–Ivory Coast* this time. Then he learned his 16 times table and his 17 times table, up to 16 times 16 and 17 times 17. At lunchtime Mr. Thomas closed the store, came up the spiral staircase and made a thick milk pudding with sugar and cinnamon. They had carrot juice with added vitamins to drink.

Now Mr. Thomas was downstairs, back in the store.

Kitty and Konrad sat at the big table in the living room. "It's easy, Konrad!" Kitty said. "Education is based on the fact that a child gets praised for doing something right. And if he does something wrong he gets scolded, or ignored. So if you're good you get praise, if you're naughty you get punishments, understand?"

Konrad did understand.

"Well, re-education is just the same but the other way around," Kitty explained. "If you're naughty you get praised, if you're good you get punished. Understand?"

Konrad understood that too.

"And your re-education has to be done very fast indeed, because it's a desperate situation . . ."

". . . which calls for a desperate remedy!" Konrad put in.

"Correct!" said Kitty.

"But what exactly am I supposed to do?" asked Konrad.

"Start by saying all the bad words you know."

"I don't know any."

"Oh yes, you do," said Kitty. "Frank shouted so many after you—you must remember some of them!"

Konrad went very red in the face. "Well, yes, but I can't say things like that! I get a funny feeling in my throat, and they won't come out."

"Try saying something good and then something bad in turn," Kitty suggested.

"Please, ma'am," Konrad started—and then he yelled "Ow!" because Kitty had pricked his arm with a pin. (This is all part of re-education.)

"M-m-meat—" said Konrad. He could get no further; it gave him that funny feeling in his throat.

"M-m—," Konrad tried again. Kitty nodded encouragingly. "Keep on trying till you can do it," she whispered.

"M-m-meathead!" Konrad finally got it out. Kitty leaned over and kissed him on the cheek. Konrad was very pleased.

"Now try 'Meathead' and 'Please, ma'am' in turn," Kitty told him. Konrad did. Every time he said "Please, ma'am" Kitty pricked his arm with the pin. Every time he said "Meathead" she kissed his cheek.

After ten minutes Konrad had stopped even wanting to say "Please, ma'am." He kept saying, "Meathead, meathead, meathead!" and getting kisses.

"That's great, Konrad!" Kitty was thrilled. "You're fantastic! You're a fast study!" Then she gave Konrad his first test. He went over to the phone and dialed a number, any number. The one he happened to dial was 757-2312. "Henderson here," said a man's voice. Konrad gulped and choked; little beads of sweat stood out on his forehead.

"Go on, say it!" Kitty whispered.

"I'm ever so sorry . . ." Konrad said into the receiver. Kitty held her pin in front of his nose. Konrad shut his eyes, gulped again, and added, ". . . you dumb meathead!" Then he hung up.

As a reward Kitty kissed Konrad on both cheeks, and she said Konrad had learned enough for one day, so they'd play a game now.

"Did you bring the quiz game with you?"

"No," said Kitty. "We're going to play at drawing on walls." She put a piece of red chalk and a piece of green chalk in Konrad's hand. Of course, Konrad did not want to draw on the walls because he thought Mr. Thomas might not like it.

"Never mind him," said Kitty enticingly. "Just think

how lovely the flowers you'd like to draw would look."

"They'd have stems like this," said Konrad—then he was horrified, because he had made a long green mark on the wall.

"Very good, Konrad! Terrific, Konrad! That's great, Konrad," said Kitty enthusiastically, putting a peppermint cream in his mouth. Konrad loved peppermint creams.

By six o'clock Konrad had eaten a whole carton of peppermint creams, and every inch of the living-room walls not already covered by a picture had flowers drawn on it.

Mr. Thomas almost had heart failure when he came upstairs after locking up and saw the flowers all over his living-room walls, but Kitty said hastily, "Desperate situations, Mr. Thomas . . ."

". . . call for desperate remedies. Yes, I know," sighed Mr. Thomas. And Konrad said, "Meathead!" to him, three times.

"You must praise him!" Kitty whispered to Mr. Thomas. "Go on, or you'll spoil all my work."

It was the hardest thing Mr. Thomas had ever been asked to do in all his life. But he bent down to Konrad. "How well you say 'Meathead,' my boy," he said. "I'm proud of you!"

For reasons of security, Kitty had decided it would be better not to visit Bertie Bartolotti. And for the same reasons, Mrs. Bartolotti had decided not to visit either Kitty or Mr. Thomas. However, Kitty and Mrs. Bartolotti were in communication. They could communicate through the bathroom ventilators. The Robertsons' bathroom was right under Mrs. Bartolotti's bathroom, and both bathrooms had ventilators ending in a square hole near the tub covered with a grating. If you spoke into the hole you could be heard in the bathroom above or below. Kitty and Mrs. Bartolotti had fixed what times they would speak to each other, every evening at seven o'clock, and during lunch at one-thirty. They arranged a procedure for urgent emergency messages too: if Mrs. Bartolotti had anything urgent to say she would hammer three nails into her kitchen wall, and if Kitty had something to say she would play her harmonica. Both sounds could be heard through the walls.

So at seven that evening Bertie Bartolotti went into the bathroom, crouched down by the ventilator shaft and called out, "Are you there, Kitty?"

"Yes," said a voice from the shaft. The ventilator altered voices a lot; Kitty's sounded like the voice of an ancient old dwarf.

"How's Konrad doing?" asked Mrs. Bartolotti.

"Great. He's a very fast study."

"The Service Department people came. A horrid little man. I threw him out!"

Mrs. Bartolotti waited for an answer, but none came. Putting her ear to the grating, she heard Mr. Robertson saying crossly, "What on earth are you doing in the bathroom all this time, Kitty?"

Mrs. Bartolotti got up, sighing sadly, because she would have liked the chance to talk to Kitty for longer. Then she went into her kitchen to cook the only egg she had left for supper. She was just wondering whether a chopped pickled herring would improve the egg when the doorbell rang. It rang twice, two long rings. Mrs. Bartolotti turned the flame low under her egg and tiptoed to the door. She had a peephole in the door with a brass flap over it, and now she pushed the brass flap aside very quietly and carefully. She was expecting to see out into the passage, and it gave her a nasty shock to find she was looking right into a bright blue eye. She jumped back in alarm. The owner of the bright blue eye, standing outside her door, must have been much less nervous by nature than Mrs. Bartolotti, because he did not jump back at all; his bright blue eye remained glued to the peephole.

"Open up, Mrs. Bartolotti," called a deep voice.

"We know you're in there," called a medium-pitched voice.

"She isn't going to open up of her own accord," said a high voice.

Good heavens above, three of them! thought Bertie Bartolotti. She looked to make sure the safety chain was on its hook, the bolt was properly closed and the key turned in the lock.

The bell rang again, three times. And the deep voice, the medium-pitched voice and the high voice all said at once, "Open up at once, Mrs. Bartolotti!"

"What do you want?" asked Bertie Bartolotti. She found it very difficult to make her voice sound loud and brave.

"We want a word with you," said the high voice.

"About the wrong delivery that you have misappropriated," said the medium-pitched voice.

"If you don't open this door at once we shall come in by force."

Bertie Bartolotti's front door was made of solid oak, her bolt was made of thick brass and her safety chain was the best stainless steel.

"You just try it!" said Mrs. Bartolotti.

The high voice, the medium-pitched voice and the deep voice did some whispering together outside the door. Then Mrs. Bartolotti heard heavy footsteps moving away, and then she heard footsteps on the stairs. She sighed with relief. She thought the footsteps were going downstairs.

"What I need now," muttered Mrs. Bartolotti, "is a dose of bitters!" The bottle of bitters was on a shelf in the kitchen. She opened the bottle and raised it to her mouth. When Bertie Bartolotti drank straight from the bottle she always had to close her eyes. After she had finished drinking she put the bottle down on the table, opened her eyes again and looked at the kitchen window. There she saw three pairs of sky-blue boots and three pairs of legs in sky-blue trousers dangling in front of the dark evening sky. First the boots were right at the top of the window frame, then they were in the middle of the window frame, and the legs were getting longer and longer, and then there were three men in sky-blue uniforms standing on the kitchen windowsill. They wore sky-blue crash helmets and silver gloves, they had silver cartridge belts slung around their hips, and silver guns in silver holsters on their belts.

Mrs. Bartolotti was even more frightened than when she had opened Konrad's can. She collapsed onto a kitchen chair. The whole kitchen, along with the three men on the windowsill, seemed to be going around in circles.

The three men spoke, in chorus. "Well, you needn't have put us to all the trouble of climbing the roof!"

Gradually the kitchen stopped going around. "Who are you, anyway?" asked Mrs. Bartolotti.

"Factory Guard!" said the three men, jumping down off the windowsill and into the kitchen.

They searched the kitchen first. Then they proceeded to search the living room and the workroom and the bedroom. They also searched the bathroom. They even dug through the cabinet in the hall.

Mrs. Bartolotti stayed sitting on the kitchen chair, calling the men names. "Thick-headed louts!" she said. "I've already told you, he ran away. Four days ago!" And, "Will you kindly get out? You're trespassing!" And, "Who gave you the right to do this kind of thing?"

The three men ignored her. They combed the apartment as carefully as if they were searching for a tiny but valuable diamond. Every now and then Mrs. Bartolotti heard the deep voice saying, "Did you ever see such a ramshackle place?" And the medium-pitched voice saying, "Disgusting!" And the high voice saying, "Quite revolting!"

Suddenly the deep voice said, "Hello, hello, hello, what's all this?"

The three men came into the kitchen and held one of Konrad's school notebooks open under Mrs. Bartolotti's nose. It was open at yesterday's work, and it was dated with yesterday's date.

"Ran away four days ago, did he?" asked the man with the high voice, sarcastically.

"Got you there, eh?" said the man with the medium-pitched voice, grabbing Mrs. Bartolotti's shoulder. But that was more than she could stand. She bit the arm of the man with the deep voice. He let out a yell, and they all let go of her.

"Come on, we've got enough proof," said the man with the high voice. "The old girl's hidden him away somewhere. Must have done it after she got the letter from the company."

The man with the medium-pitched voice closed the note-book and stuffed it inside his uniform jacket. Then the three men marched out of the kitchen and through the hall to the door of the apartment.

Mrs. Bartolotti heard them unhooking the safety chain, pushing back the bolt and turned the key in the lock. The door closed again, and their footsteps faded away.

Bertie Bartolotti picked up her hammer and drove three enormous nails into the wall. Then she ran into the bath-room and called down the ventilator shaft, "Kitty! Kitty, can you hear me?"

But Kitty did not answer. She was fast asleep. "Well, really!" said Mr. Robertson to his wife. He was sitting in the living room reading his paper. "Can't she hammer her wretched nails during the day?"

Chapter Ten ———————

The next day was a half day in school, and Kitty Robertson went off to help Joanne Miller with her tables again. Mrs. Robertson was proud of her daughter. "You're a good, helpful child," she said approvingly. Kitty nodded. Her conscience was perfectly clear; the fact that she was being helpful to Konrad Bartolotti, not Joanne Miller, didn't make any difference.

Kitty had thought up an especially good program for this afternoon. She ran up the spiral staircase to Konrad.

"How's my mother?" Konrad asked her.

"I'm deaf today," said Kitty. "Write your question down, please." She gave Konrad a crumpled bit of paper covered with grease spots, and a blunt, chewed-up pencil. Konrad hated the look of the crumpled paper and the chewed-up pencil, but since he wanted badly to know how Mrs. Bartolotti was he overcame his distaste and wrote on the nasty piece of paper:

How is my mother?

And he held it out to Kitty. Kitty looked at the writing and said, "Oh, I can't read neat handwriting like that! Make it a bit less regular, please. With some letters leaning to the right and others leaning to the left, and the lines not so straight either."

Since Konrad absolutely had to know how Mrs. Bartolotti was, he did his best to write crooked, untidy letters. He used up nine greasy, crumpled bits of paper before Kitty decided his writing was bad enough.

"Mrs. Bartolotti is doing fine," said Kitty when she had read the ninth note, and all of a sudden she could hear again. She told Konrad to sing some songs. Konrad sang, "London bridge is falling down. . . ." Kitty got a rusty old cowbell out of her pocket and rang it like mad. The noise hurt Konrad's ears, and he stopped singing. Kitty stopped ringing the bell. Konrad struck up again: "Oats, peas, beans, . . ." Kitty rang her bell. And when he tried "Here we go 'round the mulberry bush," Kitty rang like the fire brigade.

"Kitty!" shouted Konrad. "How can I sing with all that noise going on?"

"Sing the one about the burning of the school," Kitty said. Konrad didn't want to. "It isn't a nice song," he objected.

"Never mind, sing it," said Kitty.

Konrad started. "My eyes have seen the glory of the burning of the school . . ." Kitty did not ring her bell. She was humming the tune too. Konrad was so pleased the awful ringing had stopped and Kitty was humming the tune so nice and quietly that he went on, "We've tortured every teacher and we've broken every rule."

Konrad loved singing. After the song about the school he tried to sing, "Did you ever hear of sweet Betsey from Pike," but that made Kitty ring her bell again. And she rang it when he started "Oats, peas, beans and barley grow" again. But when he struck up, "We three Kings of

Orient are, tried to smoke a rubber cigar," she didn't ring her bell, she hummed the tune too, pure as an angel, clear as a bell. And when Konrad sang, "While shepherds washed their socks by night, All seated 'round the tub, A shower of Ivory soap came down, And they began to scrub," she hummed so tunefully that Konrad realized what a beautiful carol it really was, and he sang it ten times running.

After that Konrad and Kitty practiced tearing up newspapers, and sticking gum under the table, and stirring spinach into raspberry Jello. At the end of the re-education lesson Konrad had to cut all the tassels off the black silk tablecloth. It came very hard to him at first; he moaned and groaned every time he snipped off a tassel. But by the time one corner of the cloth had lost all its tassels he was not moaning so loudly. After the second corner he had stopped moaning completely, he did the third corner very easily, and the fourth corner was child's play. And when the last tassel fell to the floor Konrad actually giggled. Kitty kissed him three times on each cheek as a reward, and let him throw all the black tassels out the window. "They look like black snow!" said Konrad, giggling.

Chapter Eleven ─────────

At seven that evening, Kitty was able to tell Mrs. Bartolotti up the ventilator shaft that Konrad was making great progress. "You'd never believe how fast he's changing!" said Kitty, admiringly.

"I only hope it works," murmured Mrs. Bartolotti. Ever since the three sky-blue men had been to see her she had been feeling depressed. Kitty herself was not as confident and cheerful as she made out. She was a very observant girl, and when she left the drugstore that evening she had seen a sky-blue man standing by the door of the building, reading a paper. And who would be standing in the doorway of an apartment building on a dull evening to read his paper? Kitty thought it looked very suspicious. Then, at supper, Mrs. Robertson had said, "What do you think? A social worker came by today, wanting to know about that boy Konrad." Kitty's mashed potato fell off her fork because that gave her such a shock, and Mr. Robertson said, "Can't you eat nicely, child?"

"She wanted the address of Konrad's father," Mrs. Robertson went on. And Kitty said, "But he's gone to Katmandu!" But Mrs. Robertson said she had given the social worker Mr. Thomas's address. "Never mind about his natural father!" said Mrs. Robertson. "Konrad always told me that Mr. Thomas the druggist was his father!" At that point Kitty dropped her fork, and Mr. Robertson snapped again, "For goodness' sake, can't you eat properly?"

Kitty picked up her fork, saying, "What was the social worker wearing?"

Nor was she one bit surprised when her mother said, "Oh, some kind of blue uniform with silver buttons."

Kitty's first reaction was to play her harmonica and tell Mrs. Bartolotti all about it. But then she decided that Mrs. Bartolotti had quite enough on her mind already, and there was nothing she could actually do about it. The only person who could do anything was herself, Kitty. She must speed up Konrad's re-education.

Kitty decided not to go to school at all the next day. She would go straight to Konrad instead, and do everything she possibly could. (Kitty did not like to cut school; she was not that sort of child. But, as she said to herself, very desperate situations call for very desperate remedies.)

At nine o'clock sharp Mr. Thomas was opening up the drugstore. He saw Kitty standing outside.

"Oh, dear me, Kitty!" said Mr. Thomas quietly. "You shouldn't come as openly as this. You'll attract attention."

"Trying to hide doesn't matter now," said Kitty. "Look at that telephone booth! What can you see?"

"A man in a sky-blue uniform," said Mr. Thomas.

"And who's that at the bus stop?"

"A woman in a sky-blue coat and skirt."

"And outside the florist?"

"A man in a sky-blue suit."

"Rather a lot of sky blue for such a cloudy morning, don't you think?" said Kitty.

Mr. Thomas nodded, unhappily. Kitty pulled him inside the shop. "Do you think it's all over, then?" wailed Mr. Thomas.

"Certainly not," said Kitty. "I'm going straight up to Konrad to start my special intensive course. It'll make a lot of noise, I'm afraid."

"What shall I do?" asked Mr. Thomas. "Shall I send for Bertie? I think she's braver than me!"

Kitty thought that was a good idea. Mr. Thomas found a piece of paper and wrote. "Dear Bertie, We are in grave danger. Come at once!"

Mr. Thomas folded up the piece of paper, and saw that Mrs. Biddles, the super of the building, was sweeping the sidewalk outside his store.

"Mrs. Biddles!" called Mr. Thomas, from the door of the store. "Mrs. Biddles, would you be kind enough to take Mrs. Bartolotti this note?"

Mrs. Biddles would be kind enough. She took the note from him.

"And if you see anyone in sky blue," said Mr. Thomas, "don't give them this letter whatever you do!"

"I won't, don't you worry," said Mrs. Biddles, stumping off. Mr. Thomas and Kitty watched her go. Mrs. Biddles was going to walk past the bus stop and the sky-blue woman.

"She'll snatch the note!" wailed Mr. Thomas.

And the woman in sky blue did lay her hand on Mrs. Biddles's arm. But Mrs. Biddles whacked the sky-blue woman over the head with her broom and yelled, "Help! I'm being assaulted!" The sky-blue woman ran away.

"Mrs. Biddles has still got the note," said Kitty, relieved. She went through the three rooms in the back and up the spiral staircase.

Konrad was in the bathroom taking a shower. He was delighted to see Kitty so early. Now that she was working on his re-education he didn't seem to get much fun out of learning things from the encyclopedia anymore.

"Konrad, they know you're here!" said Kitty. "This is your last chance."

"Let's get down to work, then!" said Konrad. He was a very fast study.

At nine-thirty Bertie Bartolotti came into the drugstore. She had on even more makeup than usual, and she was wearing violet pants and a yellow blouse. Mrs. Bartolotti pretended to be dusting while Mr. Thomas stood behind the counter selling pills. She dusted all around the inside of the window frame, looking out for the sky-blue people. She recognized the one in the telephone booth; he was the man with the high voice. And the man with the medium-pitched voice was waiting outside the florist's store. And the man now standing on the corner reading his paper was the one with the deep voice. In all, Mrs. Bartolotti counted seven sky-blue people gathered around the druggist's.

At about ten o'clock the sky-blue woman from the bus stop crossed the street and came into the drugstore.

"Can I help you?" asked Mr. Thomas, in a trembling voice.

The woman handed him a prescription for some medicine that was very seldom sold, so Mr. Thomas did not have it in stock.

"I shall have to order it," said Mr. Thomas.

"Then please do," said the woman in sky-blue, looking at the ceiling in some surprise, because all three overhead lights were swaying about like mad.

Mr. Thomas rang the pharmaceutical express service, which promised to deliver it in two hours.

"If you come back in two hours I shall have it ready," said Mr. Thomas.

However, the sky-blue woman did not want to go away. She said she would prefer to wait, and she sat down on the bench where people waited for their prescriptions, looking at the swaying overhead lights and then, even more surprised, watching the glass jars on the shelves, because by now they too were jumping around and clinking together.

At about quarter past ten a sky-blue man came into the shop. He had an unusual prescription as well, and he too said he would wait. He sat down beside the sky-blue woman and stared in surprise at a damp patch on the ceiling of the room, which was slowly getting larger and darker. (Mr. Thomas's bedroom was right above the front of the store, and Konrad was in there learning how to water carpets.)

At eleven o'clock Mrs. Biddles came into the shop, very flustered.

"What do you think, Mr. Thomas?" she said. "There are two sky-blue men in the hall, and two more sky-blue men out in the yard where the garbage cans are, and whatever I say to them they won't go away!"

"We're surrounded!" whispered Mrs. Bartolotti. And the lights were swaying so wildly, and the glass jars clinking so loud, that Mrs. Biddles asked, "Is it an earthquake or something?"

"No, no," said Mr. Thomas. "Just the workmen up in my apartment." That put the super's mind at rest, and she went out of the store to go and insult the sky-blue men some more.

At half past eleven a gentleman came into the drugstore. He wore a sky-blue coat and silver-framed glasses, and he was carrying a silver briefcase. He was followed by a man in a sky-blue uniform, and the man in uniform was followed by a man and woman, obviously a married couple, dressed in gray. The wife had a little pointy nose, and the husband had a big bald spot.

The couple in gray sat down on the bench. "Very soon now you will have your son in your arms!" the gentleman with the silver-framed glasses told them.

"And about time too," said the man with the bald spot.

"You've been putting us off with promises for weeks," said the woman with the pointy nose.

Besides all the people in sky blue and the gray couple there were two perfectly ordinary customers in the shop. The man in uniform went and held the door open, shouting, "You are in acute danger of infection! Please leave the premises!" The two ordinary customers looked scared.

"Get out, quick, get out!" said the man with the silver-framed glasses, pointing to the door.

"It's a lie! There's no danger of infection here at all!" shouted Mr. Thomas.

"Oh, do stay!" cried Mrs. Bartolotti to the ordinary customers. But the man in uniform took hold of them and pushed them out the door. Then he closed it behind them and turned the notice hanging behind the glass around, so that it said CLOSED on the side you could see from the street.

"And do I get my good little boy now, may I ask?" inquired the woman with the pointy nose.

"Immediately, madam!" said the man with the silver-framed glasses. And turning to Mr. Thomas, he said, "Come along, where's that boy? He is my property. You have no right to him at all." Then he turned to Mrs. Bartolotti, adding, "As for you, you have still less, you very peculiar person!"

Then the man with the silver-framed glasses and the man in uniform tried to go through into the rooms behind the store.

"Over my dead body!" said Mr. Thomas, in a trembling voice that sounded very small and frightened.

"Don't you let him by!" called Mrs. Bartolotti. "Kick his shins!"

"Ah, but there's no need for me to fetch the boy, you know!" said the man with the silver-framed glasses, smiling. "All my Instant Children obey a command at once!" And he cupped his hands around his mouth and shouted, "Konrad!"

He shouted, "Konrad!" three more times. Then he shouted, "Konrad, come here this minute!" three times. But still Konrad did not come. The overhead lights were still swaying frantically, the glass jars on the shelves were clinking musically, and the damp patch had grown to an enormous size.

"Why isn't he coming?" asked the man with the bald spot. "We particularly ordered an obedient child!"

"Oh, he never listens to anything you say!" said Mrs. Bartolotti. "Some children are like that. You can talk till your jaws hurt, and they won't take any notice."

The pointy-nosed woman jumped up from the bench, screeching, "But the boy we ordered obeys the slightest word!"

"So he does, so he does," the man with the silver-framed glasses assured her soothingly. "Very likely there's someone up there keeping him from coming down. I expect that girl has hold of him."

The man with the silver-framed glasses pointed to the man in uniform. "You stay here and watch this door," he said. "We'll rush the upstairs rooms!" And although Mr. Thomas very bravely got in his way, and Mrs. Bartolotti, equally bravely, tried to grab the sky-blue woman's hair, the gentleman in silver-framed glasses and the sky-blue people and the couple in gray pushed their way into the back rooms. They ran through the first, and second and the third rooms behind the shop and reached the spiral staircase.

And then Konrad called out, from upstairs, "All right, all right, I'm coming down, you stupid meatheads!"

Konrad came sliding down the banister on his stomach, feet first. Since the pointy-nosed woman was standing at the end of the banister, she got both his feet right in her middle.

"Sorry, old bag!" said Konrad. "I'm afraid I did it on purpose!" Then he looked around and said, "So who was the idiot bawling for me like a pig getting its throat cut?"

The pointy-nosed woman clutched her middle and screeched, "You don't mean to say this is the boy I ordered from your factory? I wonder you're not ashamed of yourself—and you the president too!"

The president of the factory straightened his silver-framed glasses and stared at Konrad.

"Listen, you soft-boiled prune!" said Konrad. "I know a good song." And he sang, "Glory, glory, hallelujah, teacher hit me with a ruler . . ."

"Disgraceful!" cried the man with the bald spot. "Is this your idea of a well-mannered child? You're a bunch of swindlers!"

"Don't get so worked up, Baldy!" said Konrad. "Or I might cut off your mustache, and then you wouldn't have any hair left at all!"

Kitty appeared at the top of the spiral staircase and leaned over the banister. "Hungry, Konrad?" she shouted down.

"You bet!" called Konrad.

"What would you like?"

"Raspberry Jello and spinach!" Konrad shouted up.

"Coming down!" yelled Kitty, and then the sky-blue people and the president and the couple in gray took cover, because Kitty was throwing raspberry Jello and spinach down the stairway.

"We always do it like this," said Kitty. "I stand up here and he stands down there. I take a handful of spinach and he opens his mouth."

"Only she doesn't always aim too well," said Konrad.

The president of the factory took off his glasses because he couldn't see through them anymore. The left lens was covered with raspberry Jello and the right lens was covered with spinach. The president peered nearsightedly at Konrad. "Impossible!" he said. "This boy can never have been produced by our factory!"

The sky-blue people were trying to wipe splashes of food off their uniforms. The couple in gray were crouching behind a pile of empty cardboard cartons. "What a frightful child!" said the man with the bald spot.

"We'll get a dog instead!" said the pointy-nosed woman.

They got up without saying good-bye to either the president or the people in sky blue, and went off toward the front of the shop.

"What's up, boss?" called the man left to guard the door. "Why are the lady and gentleman going without their child? Why did they say we're a bunch of crooks? Hey, boss! Boss, what's up?" The man at the door was frantic.

The president had wiped his glasses, the sky-blue people had wiped the splashes of spinach and raspberry Jello off their clothes.

"Let's go!" said the president, putting on his glasses.

"What about me?" asked Konrad.

"You disgusting brat!" said the president. "You're nothing whatever to do with me!"

"Glad to hear it," said Mrs. Bartolotti, opening the back door. "Nice to have known you, ladies and gentlemen!" she shouted, as the president and the sky-blue people marched through the door.

"And kindly remove your guards from the garbage cans," said Mr. Thomas, "or Mrs. Biddles will be furious."

Kitty closed the back door behind them.

Konrad was sitting on a crate of baby food, looking very pale.

"Crimenny!" he said, "I'm bushed!"

"My poor darling!" said Mrs. Bartolotti, stroking his right cheek.

"My poor darling!" said Mr. Thomas, stroking his left cheek.

"You were wonderful!" said Kitty, and she kissed him on the mouth.

"Do I have to be like that all the time now?" asked Konrad.

"Heaven forbid!" cried Mr. Thomas.

"Do I have to be the way I was before now?" asked Konrad.

"Heaven forbid!" cried Mrs. Bartolotti.

Kitty put her arm around his shoulders. "Don't worry, Konrad, we'll get along all right!" she said.

"A beautifully wrought story of a mountain Mary Poppins."—
School Library Journal

IDA EARLY COMES OVER THE MOUNTAIN

by Robert Burch
(author of *Queenie Peavie*)

Life was rough in the Blue Ridge Mountains of Georgia, but things certainly took a turn for the lively when Ida Early came over the mountain! For the four Sutton children, Ida appeared just in time. With their mother dead, their father at work, and unpredictable Ida hired on as housekeeper, bossy Aunt Earnestine might finally go back to Atlanta.

Ida brought laughter back into the household. And the Suttons grew to love the tall tales she told at the toss of her hat. But their friendship was put to the test when the Sutton kids learned that there was more to Ida Early than just her funny ways.

An ALA Notable Book
AN AVON CAMELOT • 57091-2 • $1.95